Tim Burden

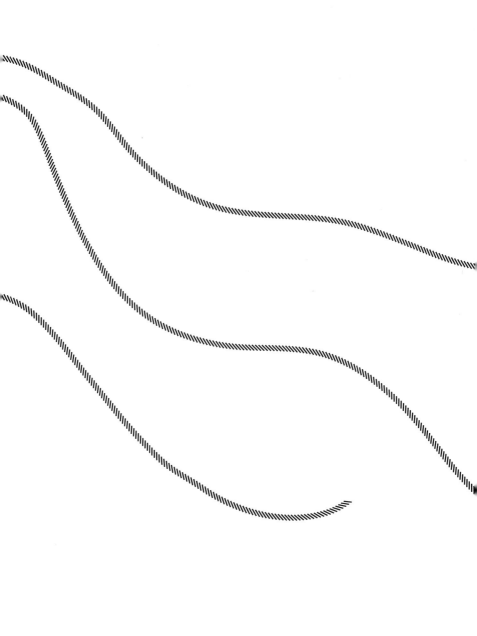

EVANGELLYFISH

DOUGLAS WILSON

canonpress
Moscow, Idaho

Published by Canon Press
P.O. Box 8729, Moscow, ID 83843
800.488.2034 | www.canonpress.com

Douglas Wilson, *Evangellyfish*
Copyright © 2012 by Douglas Wilson.

Cover design by David Dalbey.
Printed in the United States of America.

Library of Congress Cataloging-in-Publication Data

Wilson, Douglas, 1953-
Evangellyfish / by Douglas Wilson.
    p. cm.
ISBN 978-1-59128-098-9
1. Clergy--Fiction. 2. Big churches--Fiction. 3. Adultery--Fiction. 4. Satire. I. Title.
PS3623.I57875E93 2011
813'.6--dc22
                                    2011028349

13 14 15 16 17 18 19   9 8 7 6 5 4 3 2

This book is for
Aaron Rench,
who did not despair.

This is as good a place as any to insist that all the characters in *Evangellyfish* are fictional, and I made them all up out of my own head. Any resemblance to any real people, living or dead, is their own darn fault. If they quit acting like that, the resemblance would cease immediately and we wouldn't have to worry about it.

CONTENTS

FATHER CONFESSOR

I have only two comforts to live upon; the one is the perfections of
Christ; the other is the imperfections of Christians.
Nathaniel Ward, Puritan

A s a conscientious pastor, John regretted having given a
fellow clergyman a black eye. Not entirely intentional; more
a confluence of events that was larger than everybody involved.
But still, hardly what he had learned in seminary.

John Mitchell was a Reformed Baptist pastor, the sort who
drank a little, but not in front of folks from other churches, and
made sure that nothing more exciting than ping-pong happened
in the youth group. When asked what he did for a living, he
would sometimes quote *Fletch*—"I'm a shepherd." He generally
had to explain the reference, and it was never as funny as he
hoped. When asked what his degrees were in, he would say that
his undergrad was in philosophy, and he had an MDiv from
Westminster, but that everything he did was "deeply rooted in
the blues." Some people didn't get that either.

He was a man diligent in his ways and not easily discouraged. His flock was small, in a relatively large Midwestern city, and they got along well with each other. He was not the kind of pastor that any of his flock would have guessed as capable of any kind of ministerial mayhem at all.

He had gone to junior high and high school with Michelle Lester, the wife of his adversary, but had only met Chad Lester twice before the incident. The Rev. Lester, the recipient of said eye-blackening, was the leading light and chief shaman at a mega-church across town. The two congregations, and the two men, were in the same city, but they existed in entirely different realities. Pastor Mitchell had the advantage of his reality being more or less real. Chad Lester, by way of contrast, had some time ago opted out of reading his moral compass with any reference to true north. Having inscribed directions on the edges of your moral compass, and a needle that works, was entirely too confining.

Pastor Mitchell was sitting quietly in his study after dinner, scratching his gray beard. It had been twenty-four hours since— as the diplomats would phrase it—the frank exchange of views had taken place. His knuckles were still throbbing gently. Cherie, his wife's cousin, had panicked at him over the phone, and he had hurried over to her condo, unsure what the problem was. He surprised, and was in turn surprised by, Chad Lester, who was there with Cherie trying to . . . well, it was not at all clear now what he had been trying to do. But Mitchell had *thought* at the time he knew what Lester was trying to do. Words had been exchanged, including some bits of high-volume exegesis and penetrating theological insight. Chad had stumbled on his way to the door, lurching into Mitchell, and Mitchell had taken that opportunity to unload a punch which connected with a less-than-perfect tenderness. But as punches go, analyzed merely in the interests of dispassionate science and apart from any ethical considerations, it had been exquisite.

Afterward, Chad had straightened up, looked at him with an expression that Mitchell had interpreted as a spiritual rebuke *in excelsis,* and then staggered out the front door, his hand over his eye. The look he directed at Mitchell had actually been a look which simply acknowledged receipt of a complete novelty, but Mitchell had a tender conscience, and under the circumstances couldn't be expected to know that. Mitchell felt, down in his soul he felt, that Lester saw him as a hypocrite. And to have someone like *Lester* look down on him for hypocrisy was just the utter, frozen limit. But it seemed that Lester, if he thought that, would have a *point,* would he not? Gkkk.

So here he was, a day later, playing teeter-totter in his soul, going back and forth about what he ought to do. He really was a humble man, and did not mind seeking forgiveness where necessary. He had done so many times in his life, most recently for calling a young man a buffle-headed young dope during a counseling appointment. But this thing was different. Asking that man's forgiveness would involve *talking* with him, and talking to Lester was about as much fun as fishing in an outhouse. Of course, Mitchell had what a strict recording angel would have called "ample grounds" for all his reluctance to talk with Lester, but he was still worked over by the whole thing. He did know that his feelings for Lester went somewhat beyond the legal limits of righteous indignation. After what Lester had done to Cherie years before, and to all the other women Mitchell knew about—and then factor in the ones he didn't know about—the end result was a stew that Mitchell felt to be quite beyond his capacities to eat. But there was e-mail. He could e-mail an apology.

The phone rang, and John stared at it balefully. He glanced at the clock—it was a little before seven, and he had to leave about quarter after for his daughter's volleyball game. They were playing at some obscure Christian school—he thought it must be a Christian school with a name like Joppa—located on a street he had never heard of before. He had given himself fifteen extra minutes for getting lost and found again, but he did not really have any time to chew up on the phone. It rang again, and John pursed his lips and picked it up, hoping it wasn't Deidre Hannock. She was a solo-obsessed soprano in their makeshift choir and was always calling with criticisms of the choir director disguised as prayer requests. Mitchell's mother had always called church choirs the war department. Luther once said that when Satan fell, he fell into the choir loft. Please don't let it be Deidre . . .

"Mitchells'."

But the voice was low, nowhere close to soprano, and kind of slurred.

"Hello, Pastor Mitchell?"

"Speaking."

"This is Chad." This was followed by what sounded like the *thup thup thup* sound of sobbing.

John Mitchell lurched forward in his chair, and without thinking, pulled open one of the drawers of his desk. *What am I doing?* he thought. *Looking for rubber gloves? A gas mask? Grace? No grace in* there. *None around here anywhere.*

"What do you want?" he said.

"I . . . I need help," the voice said.

Instinct and long experience nudged Pastor Mitchell, poking him helpfully on the shoulder. "Have you been drinking?" he asked.

"Sort of," Chad said. "I have never done anything like this before. I need help. I couldn't think of anyone else to call."

"I punched you in the eye. What makes you think I would help you?"

"You're a pastor. It's a brotherhood. I really need—" A crash cut Chad off.

"Chad? Lester?"

"Sorry. I just tripped."

"Where are you?" John asked. He knew he was stalling.

"I am at the Hyatt. Room 306. Just a second." A couple of moments went by with the sound of a door opening and then closing again. "Yeah, 306. You should come here. I can't drive."

"You're drunk, and you want me to come over there? You don't want my kind of help, Chad. You really don't. I can give you all

I got right now. Stop drinking, stop screwing around, repent to your congregation, and resign your pastorate."

"I don't usually drink." Chad was crying again, schlupping all over the phone.

"And read your Bible," John added. "Start now. I'm sure the Gideons left you one."

"John, please."

"Sorry, Chad. My daughter's got a volleyball game." He took the sobbing away from his ear and looked at the phone. With one lonely beep, Lester was gone, and the room was silent.

John Mitchell just sat in his chair, trying not to think. Scenes from dozens of bad movies played through his head. Villains dangling from balconies, cliffs, various ledges, villains calling out for help. Then there was John Mitchell, pastor, follower of Christ, busily stepping on their fingers. Hanging up on the tax collectors and prostitutes. He glanced at his watch and stood up, trying to embrace the role of dutiful father—*gotta get to my daughter's volleyball game*—but it didn't wash. Joppa was a small school, and Sandy's coach was almost certainly going to play the B squad. Sandy was varsity. She had told him specifically that he would be wasting his time if he came, but that she'd still love to see him going above and beyond the call of duty. He had perfect liberty to go talk to Lester, and he knew it. He had made all her other games, the ones she had actually played in. He knew he should go see Lester, but deep within the recesses of his rib cage, an insistent voice was loudly maintaining something along the lines of, "I don't wanna!"

John Mitchell started down the hallway to go say goodbye to Cindi, his wife, but then remembered that she was at a ladies' fellowship. So he wheeled around, and clumped dejectedly out the front door to the driveway. Hopping in, he started his truck up, put it savagely in gear, and pulled out into the street. He would have to decide right or left at the corner, and he didn't want to decide *anything*.

By the time he got to the corner, it had occurred to him that he could also make his final decision closer to the freeway, so for the time being he turned left and headed off for Joppa Christian. What kind of group would name their school after a Philistine seaport? What was with that? He decided that he needed to be on his toes and keep an eye on the home crowd. He might learn something new about yet another little odd church group, and he settled in a little more comfortably to the idea of watching a volleyball game.

He took the freeway and found the school with no trouble at all. It was a little cinder-block affair, with a larger steel gym right next to it. All the parking was on the street, so he found a spot and walked glumly in. The teams were both warming up. Sandy saw him, waved happily, and trotted over to greet him. She kissed him on the cheek. "Thanks for coming," she said. "Coach just told us for sure that we won't be playing. They're playing the bench for sure. If you have to do something, please go."

John found himself chafing at her generosity, and wanted her to be a bit more clingy and needy and demanding. If his daughter was a big mess, like Lester, then he would have a parental duty to stay and to not step on *her* fingers. No, he didn't want that. But he managed to say, "I might. Thanks."

He started up into the bleachers, and then realized that he needed to use the men's room. He glanced at the clock and walked out into the hallway that connected the gym to the school. Nothing there. The doors to the school were open, and a wide hallway opened up to the right. He could hardly see, but close to the entrance he could make out that the first door on the left was a ladies' room, and there were a couple doors beyond that, deeper in the gloom. He walked to the second one, opened it, and stepped in, fumbling for a light. The door clicked shut behind him, and he kicked a hard metallic object at his feet. He turned around and tried the door. Locked. Groping to the left and right, all he found were janitor's overalls, or what he judged to be something very much like janitor's overalls. He just stood there for a moment, flummoxed.

A pipe! *I smoke a pipe.* He reached into his jacket pocket, pulled out a lighter, and flicked it. He had just bought the thing yesterday, so he had plenty of fluid, while recognizing at the same time that *plenty* is a relative term. He looked around at his warm little broom closet, and then looked at the offending doorknob. Had he been there just the day before, he would have witnessed the janitor, a man named Earl—not that it matters—warning the principal about the doorknob. "Lot of little kids in this school. We have to replace that thing." The principal had nodded his sage agreement.

But this well-intentioned administrative desire did nothing to help John Mitchell out. He continued to look around, noting that the object he had kicked coming in was a mop bucket on wheels. He shouted a few times and then realized that it would likely do little good. So he grabbed the handle of the mop and began to tap it on the door, insistently and regularly. Anybody in the hall would have to come and check out such a noise. He would just be here a few minutes.

Half an hour later, still tapping, his mind began to drift in a typological direction. In seminary, he'd had very little use for that kind of stuff, and had not really paid much attention. As he put it when asked, extravagant exegesis was not his bag. But here he was, and it was kind of creepy. He did not want Chad Lester to do anything but self-destruct, just like Nineveh was supposed to. And he had run off just like Jonah had. And here he was in Joppa. But what was supposed to be Tarshish in this deal? And was he going to be here three days and three . . . Suddenly the door popped open, and a worried-looking woman with a kindly face peered in, her hair done up in a tight, fundamentalist bun. "Are you all right?" she asked.

John Mitchell stepped out into the hallway, brushing his jacket, as if to get the closet darkness off. "I'm fine, thanks so much." They laughed together for a moment about it, she made a mental note to talk with the janitor about the doorknob *again,* he thanked her effusively, and they parted friends and comrades. John went into the next door, which really was the men's room, emerged a few moments later, and walked straight out the double doors to where he had parked. The Hyatt was a couple miles south.

/ / / / / /

Chad Lester was sitting at the small hotel room table, staring at the bottles in front of him. He had no idea how to go about it, but he was still laboring manfully away. There was a small platoon of alcoholic soldiers standing there, waiting to give up their lives. "Hail, Caesar! We who are about to die salute you." There was a bottle of bourbon, one of vodka, a six-pack of beer, and (he really didn't know what he was doing) a bottle of tawny port. He had just walked around that section of the store, grabbing items at random. Where was Mitchell? He had downed a bottle of beer and several shots of bourbon since he had called. He felt like calling again, but did not trust himself to try to make it to the phone. And the concept of specific phone numbers was starting to slip beyond his grasp.

A knock at the door brought Lester partway out of the fog that was descending upon him. "Minute!" he yelled. He staggered past the bed without toppling over on it, and then navigated his way past the television, which was filling his room up with hotel porn. He had turned that on out of habit when he had checked in and, also out of habit, ceased to be aware of it. He got to the door, fumbled with the latch, and pulled it open. John Mitchell was standing there, and Chad tried to beam in a welcoming manner. John took a sudden step backwards. "Yikes!" he said. It was quite a shiner.

"In, in," Lester said, motioning helplessly with his right hand. "Where have you been, you pastoral bastard? You said you were coming."

John bit his lip and came slowly in the door before making his way over to the whiskey table to sit down. When he got next to the television, he jumped and looked around for the remote. When he found it, he turned the flesh tube off and stared angrily at Chad Lester, who was just standing there, expressionless. "What is *that* for?" John asked. "Are you trying to get an appetite for dinner by watching people chew with their mouths open?" Chad Lester just blinked at him, not comprehending.

A slow moment passed while the two men made their way to their chairs, moved them around a bit, and then sat down. Chad was being a little bit slower on the motor skills front, and so John waited patiently for him. And by "waited patiently," John had been a pastor long enough to know it meant he was actually waiting impatiently. Whenever he was waiting patiently, he didn't notice that he was waiting patiently, and John was noticing.

Chad finally eased down, did not miss the chair, and looked across the table at John with an air of minor triumph. For his part, John knew he had to be there, but he was not yet glad about it. Apart from his detestation of Lester, there was also the pastoral folly of counseling drunks. He had learned *that* lesson years before—like sweeping water uphill. But here he was. What was he supposed to say? Yet forty days and the Hyatt will fall down? What he did say was, "Well, you called." He did not add, "I'm waiting," because that would have sounded impatient.

Chad was grinning at him with his puffy cheeks and bloodshot eyes. "I knew you'd come," he said. "Guys like you have to come. The better-than-you boys always come. Like the ambulance."

NYLON STRAP AND WINCH

Christian, n. One who believes the New Testament is a divinely inspired book admirably suited to the spiritual needs of his neighbor. One who follows the teachings of Christ in so far as they are not inconsistent with a life of sin.
Ambrose Bierce, *The Devil's Dictionary*

TWO WEEKS BEFORE THE BLACK EYE, and counting . . .
Things were not supposed to unravel this way. Not this way. Some other way, maybe. Perhaps even inevitably some other way. But this charge is *false*. Reckless. Not on the menu. Deeply and profoundly unfair.

Chad Lester leaned against the inside of his office door, the newspaper sticking to his sweating hands. A secretarial heads-up had reached him just half an hour ago, and he had stopped to pick up the paper on his way in. Front page and above the fold. The last time that had happened, he'd been wearing an apron at a soup kitchen. Why hadn't the paper called him? He'd just golfed with Bryan three weeks ago. Area minister accused in sex scandal. His picture lurked in a tiny smudge box right next to another picture in a tiny smudge box. Who the hell was *that*?

Never used to even think profanities, but a whole string of them were lining up now.

"Robert P. Warner II," the caption said. Chad forced himself to read through the article again. He had never heard of the gentleman in question. Not only had he never heard of the gentleman in question, but he knew he was innocent of all charges, whatever they might happen to be, because he had never ever been with *any* gentleman in question. Why would God allow this? Deeply and profoundly unfair.

To be honest, Chad thought, between deep calming breaths—a technique he had picked up at his wife's birthing class—there was some material lying around in his life out of which a sex scandal could be assembled. But all that material involved different chromosomes. He muttered fiercely to himself, "I'm not . . . gay."

An all-knowing but disinterested observer might have said that the Rev. Lester was a compulsive sexual predator. *Call me Chad, no need to stand on ceremony here. We have an informal approach to worship. We do church* differently *here. This is not your grandmother's church.* Compulsive sexual predator? Call-me-Chad wouldn't have put it to himself that way, of course, but fair was fair, and he was an average red-blooded male, with perhaps above average red-blooded male problems. What could he say? He and King David both. Chad had slept with quite a number of women who did not have the last name of Lester, but it's not like he was even in Solomon's league. A friendlier age would have simply called them concubines, except maybe the married ones. He wasn't sure what they should be called.

Some less-than-positive facts about his sexual monkeyshines were out there, certainly. And there were more than a few participants in these irregular ecclesial liaisons who were women from his own congregation. But, Chad reasoned compellingly to himself, people relate better to ministers who have their own deep personal struggles. Women especially. Empathy? Is empathy the word? There was probably a way to make it all seem kind of tawdry, and Chad would not have been surprised if the front page of the newspaper had headlined some accusation or other from some of these women. He had been more than a little braced for *that* for years, and the dozen or so church payoffs to various women had headed off more than one close call. Most of the women he had been with had not needed payoffs, but he had the resources available for those who did. Miguel Smith, the church's CFO and Chad's personal-accountability-of-sorts confidant, had been most cooperative. There is a friend that sticks closer than a brother. Is that Proverbs? Not sure. The writers would know. They'd put it in a sermon once, and he'd made a note to remember it.

But all these mutually affirming relationships—though some had been mutually affirming for less than half an hour—had one thing in common: the nature of Chad Lester's undecalogue-like activities had been extensively and exclusively hetero. He was straight. Straight and narrow. He didn't leave that path, at any rate, imagining it as a point of pride. He just found special visitors along the way—in the ditches, good Samaritan-like. Not all of the women had been beaten and robbed by others, though some had been. But all of them had been in need. He had merely met needs, lots of needs. He had needs too, and some of those women had needed to meet needs, needed to be needed, if only as a needy recipient. It had probably even helped some of their marriages. And now here was this guy named Robert leering out at him from the front page of the smudgy, damn newspaper! Roberta was a possibility. There might have been a Roberta. But there had certainly never been a Robert P. Warner, the First *or* Second. Chad Lester cursed his way through the article again and resolved to stop swearing. *Keep yourself clean, Chad. Think it, and you'll say it; say it, and you'll say it at the wrong time. Be above reproach, untouchable.* He cursed loudly, a whole string of rather awkward and unpracticed words.

Fifteen minutes later, externally composed, his executive voice summoned his secretary into his office to take a memo. "Sharon," he said, "I need you to send an e-mail to the leadership team. Schedule an emergency meeting for this afternoon."

Sharon Atwater took down the notes for the e-mail, marveling at the confidence that radiated from Chad's voice like heat from a stove. *Unshaken. He* had *to be shaken. But he didn't sound shaken. Chad could be president. Cool customer. Don't know how he does it. What a talented toad.* She had read the article already and knew as completely as he did that the charge was false, but she had thought he would at least have been shaken. She'd looked forward to him being shaken. He wouldn't like being called gay.

A good portion of the permanent staff knew something of Chad Lester's tomcatting. Chad knew that some of the staff knew, and Sharon knew more than most, and she knew more than he thought she did. On a night during her first year attending the church, the last night of an older singles retreat, she herself had even made the great sacrifice to Chad Lester's virility in the back seat of his BMW. And there had been another incident in her first year working at the church, to the point of an all-night-long indiscretion. Chad had been all aura then— charisma, smiles, and eyes that penetrated what you thought at first was your soul, but then just turned out to be your clothes. And so if the nearby riverboat casino had been taking bets on the subject, she would have laid long odds against any Robert being one of Chad Lester's incidents.

Sharon was two years away from having saved enough money to get out, get out, get out, and of her eleven years of service— twelve, if you include her early informal role—all but six months had been fraught with cynicism. Having been burned, she was almost entirely skeptical. She was probably the only church secretary in that region of the country who would call herself (but only *to* herself) an atheist. And she had been chaste since then. An atheist evangelical nun. *Chaste* is a much better word than *sour*.

Hang tight. Just two years. Back to Tennessee.

/ / / / / /

"You see the paper?"

"I most certainly did."

"Think the prosecutor saw it?"

"You kidding? He doesn't *say*, but he wants to run for governor. The average newspaper reader doesn't know how to spell his name yet. Not that I blame them. Radavic. It's his own Yugoslavian fault. What's with that? My desk phone is going to ring within fifteen minutes. No way to avoid it. I am resigned to the will of Zeus."

The two detectives sat in the gray, formica lounge at the station, each holding a stained mug of coffee. Daniel Rourke was the veteran, and Mike Bradford wasn't. They got along all right and made a decent team. Bradford was a quick study, and Rourke knew the department rules up and down, how real non-departmental police work was done, up and down, and was on the honest side of not too scrupulous. They had been together for a year and a half and had done some good police work together. At least that's how the chief put it on the last round of evals.

Bradford grinned. "What's he gonna say?"

"He will express his concern that Robert P. Warner should have had to bring the charges before the public in this way. Allow me to summarize for you what our boss man will think and/or say: 'No individual citizen should ever carry that kind of weight alone. Newspaper interview's not the way to go. Civil suit's not the way to go. As a prosecutor I am a public servant, and I have a solemn responsibility. Prosecutors have a thankless task, but all very serious anyways. Nosy reporters. Ecclesiastical misdoings. Furrowed brow. We cannot let this kind of thing happen here in our community. I want you to open a file on this, Detective Rourke, and pay yourselves a visit to Camel Creek Community Church.'"

"Huh." Bradford got up and filled his coffee again. Rourke's phone rang, and as Rourke headed out into the hall, Bradford yelled after him, "You've been reading Nostradamus!"

Bradford stared at the formica for five minutes and picked at his teeth with an unwound paper clip until Rourke came back in. Rourke said, "That was Radavic. It was all there except for the furrowed brow part. On that point I shall remain undecided. The phone has its limitations. But his brow *sounded* furrowed."

Bradford nodded. "Well, let's go. I haven't been to a church since Easter."

"I was there last week, and my priest is going to be really happy about this. Finally, the Protestants are doing their part to get the heat off us. True Christian unity is a wonderful thing. That's what he will say. He'll probably send Lester a card."

/ / / / / /

At five to three, the leadership team of Camel Creek silently began to assemble in the executive meeting room. On the wall opposite the two doorways was a small bulletin board. In the upper left-hand corner was a motivational poster, a retro image from a lost world. A soft-faced woman in a pink uniform and apron was handing a hobo a milkshake on the sidewalk in front of a 1950s diner. But behind the hobo, semitransparent, stood another figure, a figure with a clean beard wearing a sheet and smiling approvingly with his blue eyes. "It's great to serve the KING" sprawled across the bottom. Chad had designed it himself, and had actually made a lot of money on it. A copy of it was in virtually every room of the entire church complex, and it wallpapered most of the computers.

Those who arrived early were silent, shifting nervously in their seats, and all their customary business-traveler-in-the-hotel-lobby chatter was absent. There were quiet hugs, tears, and a few murmured exhortations to prayer. A Christian man was being fed to the hungry lions. Persecution never rests. Eleven men and women, not counting Chad, were expected. Along the mahogany table, at each place, Sharon Atwater had placed a blank notepad, a sharpened pencil, a copy of the newspaper article, and a roll of Testamints®. A matching mahogany box cover for some Kleenex was in the middle of the table, and a pitcher of water and ice was down at the far end. The thick carpet muffled the sounds of the few greetings that were exchanged, and finally, when all were there, Chad motioned for them to sit. Sharon sat in the corner with a notebook on her knees.

"Miguel," Chad said. "Why don't you read something from the Word and open us up with prayer?"

Miguel had just seen Hebrews 13:1 on another poster at the church radio station, and it seemed like just the ticket. Two hands holding in the foreground, and a roaring California sunset as the backdrop. Unfortunately, the poster had not let him know what to expect in the following verses. He picked up a copy of *The Message* on a side table and found the place. The elder board all joined hands and looked down at the table like they were bowing their heads. Miguel cleared his throat and began.

"Stay on good terms with each other, held together by love [*so much for the poster*]. Be ready with a meal or a bed when it's needed. Why, some have extended hospitality to angels without ever knowing it! Regard prisoners as if you were in prison with them. Look on victims of abuse as if what happened to them had happened to you. Honor marriage, and guard the sacredness of sexual intimacy between wife and husband. God draws a firm line against casual and illicit sex."

His voice faltered at the reference to prison as well as the bit about God drawing a firm line. Prisons and firm lines were a bad combination in his book. But he soldiered through anyway, and then said a quick prayer. *Why do these things happen to me anyhow? Have to stop looking at those stupid posters. But at least I'm not Chad.*

When Miguel was done, Chad lifted his prematurely gray executive head, from long habit murmured a belated *amen* that everyone could hear, and looked slowly around the room.

"Brothers, sisters. I do not need to tell you the charge is monstrous and false. The enemy is a roaring lion, seeking someone to devour. We have a good deal of work to do in finding out where this charge comes from, and what the point of it is. I confess that I am entirely baffled. You know me. We are close companions on this leadership team, and we have labored together in this vineyard for a number of years. We shall weather this together, and whatever doesn't break us makes us stronger. At the same time, we need to make a plan."

Michael Martin, the associate pastor, was studying the table closely. Wood grain was actually a fascinating study. Martin was the second-string pastor, right behind Chad Lester, but appearances can sometimes be misleading. There are times when the second-string NFL quarterback is the second-best quarterback in the whole league. Martin had all the strengths and weaknesses of Lester, though Lester had a step on him in both categories. Robert P. Warner II didn't sound very familiar to him, but it would still be prudent to check the counseling logs. This thing could blow up regardless of who did or did not do whatever to whom. *Whatever does not break us might be content with maiming us and leaving us in a ditch outside of town. Nothing to drink but ditch water. Three miles to town. Maimed, can't walk. Metaphor way too swollen. Reel it in, Martin.*

The other elders of the church were gazing steadily at the pastor. About half of them knew about him and his hormonal hobbies, but the problem was that they knew these facts through their very similar activities with most of the same women—women who happened to be talkative in bed. All people struggle with temptation. Christians aren't perfect, just forgiven. And some of the indiscretions had been forgiven for *years* now. True, others had only been forgiven for weeks. And others were ongoing, with requests for forgiveness not yet entering the picture. But still, that doesn't affect the theology of the thing. They would be forgiven eventually.

Of the four women elders there, two of them had been among the women in question. It was all very complicated, but nevertheless resulted in a remarkable unanimity. They knew he was innocent because they were as guilty as he was. *That* won't fly at a press conference, but it certainly helps maintain perspective. If they have the goods on him, he has the goods on them, and none of the goods involve a Robert P. Warner anyhow. *How can I protect myself?* was the interrogative thought of the hour floating around in about seven of the minds present, although one of the earthier elders, Kenneth by name—not that it matters—was expressing it to himself in terms of covering his white little evangelical hinder parts. The remaining four elders were confident of their pastor's innocence for all the normal reasons, and they looked at him expectantly, waiting for the next reassuring evangelical cliché, like so many show poodles waiting for their treat. Still, they were unsettled the way naive people always are when dealing with slander. How could these things be? It must be the last days. Sign of the times. Did this happen in *Left Behind*? Godly men attacked. No provocation at all.

Stephanie Nelson, a slender, five-foot-seven-inch, happily and naively married brunette, was hit the hardest. Her very attractive but forty-five-year-old eyes were filled with tears. In this dark and sinful world, the godly minister can have no rest. When the meeting was over, she hugged Chad around the neck and held him tightly for a count of thirty seconds or more, her breasts comforting his ribs. "I'm praying," she murmured as she released him, and for the first time Chad wondered if even Stephanie might have needs lying around unmet. But she didn't look back. There was no hint that she was anything but genuine.

Most of the leadership team left rapidly. Although they were quick about it, it would be too strong to say that they scurried. One of the elders, named Bill Turner, stopped at the door and then turned back to address his wife, another elder.

"Mary, you coming?"

"I'll meet you at the car in fifteen minutes. David and I have to set up a meeting with the attorneys, and David has to call his lawyer friend to see if he can be there."

"Got it." Bill tried to nod sagely and seemed immediately aware that the effect was inadequate. He then wandered aimlessly down the hall, a good metaphor for how he did most things, trying to stretch a brief return to his office to pick up a few things into fifteen minutes.

David got up and slowly shut the door, and Mary stood up and kissed him on the neck.

"Well, we're cooking in old grease now," he said. "Whatever that means."

"Yes, well, we are alive in interesting times."

"Mary, I have to tell you something. You know that you are the love of my life, my sun, my stars, my . . . you know. But before you were the love of my life, there were, um, others."

"You're not astonishing me yet."

"I am saying this because I happen to know that our minister's proclivities would not bear up well if subjected to close scrutiny. And it looks to me as though close scrutiny is on the way. Several of the women I foolishly thought at the *time* were the love of my life told me about Chad. There were at least two . . ."

Mary raised her hand. "Make that three."

"Oh, well. I see." David looked momentarily surprised. "Now the problem is not that Chad as an individual might blow up under scrutiny. I have heard rumors that three . . . um, might be a low number."

"Perhaps we have heard the same rumors."

"Yes. Well, this means that the approaching scrutiny must be directed in appropriate and edifying directions by us. On grounds of principle, I am unalterably opposed to indiscriminate scrutiny."

"And there, love, we entirely agree." She kissed him on the cheek. "See you tomorrow after the worship committee meeting? Don't forget your little blue friend this time."

/ / / / / /

Chad Lester sat down behind his desk and put his head in his hands. The meeting had gone well. No revolts. No sign of revolt. He knew about the ones who knew about him, and everyone seemed willing to be on the same team. Wouldn't do to turn on each other. Mutual interests in this one. Got a committee to deal with the press, and he'd steered the right elders to that committee. Stephanie wanted to be on it. Close call. David Lindsey has a high-octane-powered attorney friend, and he will sound him out about any possible interest in this case. In the meantime, the regular legal staff can do all the preliminary spade work. Miguel had clearly picked up on the hint to double-check with all the current feminine pension-holders to let them know that silence would indeed be fruitful. Miguel is a rock. Integrity to count on. So little integrity these days. Sign of the times. Chad lifted his head and sat back in his chair.

If anyone had cared to look through the office door at that moment, they would have seen a magisterial executive, leaning back in his leather magisterial chair. Actually, they would have seen a magisterial executive in a Hawaiian shirt. They don't stand on ceremony at Camel Creek. But even the bright floral print could not obscure the weariness from the fight. Scars from the battle on the forearms and hands of the warrior. Poured out like a drink offering. Sunbeams streamed through the slats of the well-adjusted blinds, spotlighting tiny motes wrapping up a hard day of dancing. Rich wood and thankless ministry. Polycarp. Augustine. Calvin. Hybels. No one knows loneliness like a bishop.

The picture framed by the doorway was a perfect one. Sharon Atwater walked by once and saw it. Didn't believe in it anymore, but she could still see it. Something welled up in her throat. She wondered what it was. Respectful hatred? But there was something else there as well. She was impressed. He had been impressive in that meeting. She got back to her desk and kicked herself sharply on the ankle. Don't be *stupid*.

Chad's great gift was that of being able to contain and almost completely suppress that internal sense of weightlessness and panic that he kept in an isolated chamber somewhere in the nether regions of his gut. This time the panic was a category hitherto unknown to him, and yet the view from the hallway was one of steely-eyed serenity in the face of leonine persecutors. Bulls of Bashan round about. But this was panic on stilts and steroids. This was a prison riot. The noise from that isolated chamber down below grew more insistent. A metal cup raked across the·bars. *Guards!* And somewhere farther up, unseen clammy hands were industriously attaching a nylon strap and winch around the upper portion of Chad's chest and ratcheting it tight.

Robert P. Warner! It made no *sense.* Panic about things that made sense was one thing, but panic in a world gone mad? All his gifts were extended. All his instincts had crawled out to the skinny branches to see what was coming down the road. Nothing. Made no sense at all. How was he supposed to apply the seven effective secrets of the purpose-driven CEO to *this?* How do you charisma your way out of false charges? People thought he was gay? How could they think he was gay? He wouldn't have been surprised if the world found out about all the *women,* but gay? Any woman who looked at him would know better. God was supposed to judge you for things you did, not for things you didn't. *And* He was supposed to do it at the end of the world, not in the middle of your damn . . . in the middle of your life—when things had been going so well too. Deeply and *profoundly* unfair.

Michelle would just laugh at him. The divorce was not final. You would think she would show some sympathy. They were still technically married. Shouldn't there be at least some technical sympathy?

Just like her too. No sense talking about it. She knows there were never any Roberts. Tense. Way too tense. Got to let off some steam. Stop at the fitness club on the way home and burn it all off. And despite his best counseling efforts, Bob and Erica had finally split up. Erica's new apartment was just a couple or three blocks from his club.

GANGLION MINISTRIES

If you wish to drown, do not torture yourself with shallow water.
Bulgarian proverb

THE TWO DETECTIVES STOMPED their way up the river rock steps of Camel Creek Community Church. The landscaped slopes on either side of the broad steps were covered with junipers, which Rourke had long considered to be the orcs of the plant kingdom. The automatic sprinklers on a timer were busily spritzing them, which just made them wet, botanical orcs. The two men stopped at the top step, turned around, and looked at the parking lot they had just escaped. Twenty acres of asphalt stretched out in front of them, tastefully interrupted with enclaves of trees and bushes.

"There might be more asphalt over the horizon but the curvature of the earth makes it tough to tell," Bradford said. Rourke ignored him.

They had called the previous day to arrange for interviews. A cheery voice on the other end had greeted them (almost convincingly) with, "It's great to serve the King! How may I direct your call?" Everyone was most cooperative. After the call from the prosecutor forced them to set up interviews at the church, Rourke had gone off to tie up the details of their previous case— which meant taking off early to wash his wife's Civic—and had told Bradford to make himself knowledgeable about all things Camel Creek. This, Bradford had done with a considerable amount of wicked enthusiasm, and he was bursting to show off what he had learned.

"See that?" Bradford pointed to a line of five shuttles parked off to the right. "Guess what those are for." Since Rourke was not being chatty, Bradford continued merrily. "Those are shuttles to run people in from the far end of the parking lot."

Rourke started muttering. "My church has a little lawn in front of it that takes me ten minutes to mow. And that's if I have to do any weed whacking around the Holy Mother. I'm on the mowing committee, you know. Three years. What this place must look like Sunday morning!"

"Sunday? Why limit anything to Sunday morning? Services start Friday night. One on Friday night, one on Saturday night, and three Sunday morning. Three to ten thousand people a pop, depending on the service. This guy must be good."

"What's that?" Rourke pointed to a cluster of buildings off to the right.

Bradford looked down at the map he had printed off the church website. "That," he said with satisfaction, "is King's Academy Christian School, K–12. Six hundred students or thereabouts."

"Very good, Bradford. You will go far. Knowing how to read is crucial in detective work. And that?" Behind the school's campus, on a wooded hill sloping away, were several small buildings in modeled cinder brick, with a pile of electronics on the roof. They looked like Russian fishing trawlers off Long Island at the height of the Cold War, antennae everywhere.

"Radio station K-I-N-G. Serving the King—get it?—since 1995. I spent the evening last night listening to it. They told me to 'Tune in to the KING' a bunch of times. 'He's always broadcasting,' but apparently my heart hasn't been listening. After a couple hours my wife wanted a divorce. I told her *no.* The station had a number for her to call about such things, but she wouldn't."

Rourke turned slowly. "What about this half of the world? What does the left side of the parking lot have for us?"

A small, red colonial job was nestled up close to the main sanctuary. It looked like a bank in the old city of some East Coast town that had architectural restrictions on new buildings. A little, white cupola sat perkily on the roof, and the detectives could see, even at this distance, that the place had *way* too many curtains. Open the front door, and the foofyness would just tumble out onto the front porch.

"That's New Hope Crisis Pregnancy Center."

"Huh. And what is that serious piece of work?" On the far side of the pregnancy center was an office park arrangement, with multiple buildings, walkways, and trees that were too big for the age of the buildings.

"Completing our tour of the external grounds, we see here the headquarters of TrueLife publishers. Lester's first book took off like a rocket ship and gave something called *The Prayer of Jabez* a run for its money, and we're talking about a *New York Times* bestseller-list kind of run for its money. His first book was, um . . ." Bradford looked at his papers again. "There it is. *Secrets of the Passionate Disciple*." Bradford grinned. Rourke didn't, and Bradford stopped.

They both turned around and looked at a vast array of glass doors that led to the main building. "Don't you hate it when they do that?" Bradford said. "On weekdays, which one is unlocked? Probably the last one we check."

"From what you have described about this joint so far, I would bet they're all unlocked all the time. A locked door would imply some kind of value judgment. Might turn away a seeker after Jesus." The first one they tried was unlocked, and Bradford checked one on each side. Both unlocked.

"This way, *Detective* Bradford."

The atrium was like the one in the upscale mall on the north side of town. The two men walked along the concourse, shoes clicking loudly. Past the food court. *Food* court. Then a bookshop. Then a music store. Lights were on, and people were in there. Quite a few people were in there. Skylights above let in just the right amount of mall light, gracefully falling down upon the mall cobblestones. Down the center of the concourse was a row of faux-stately mall trees. The detectives reached the end of the mall area, and Bradford started to head back.

"What are you doing?" Rourke asked.

"We must have missed the Victoria's Secret. I was going to pick up a little something for the wife. Make up for that radio station business. Lacy things can avert divorce."

"Or get you one, depending on who they're on. But I doubt your wife would want anything with a Jesus fish on it."

They both laughed and turned to look at the wall in front of them. There, in a mounted glass case, was the mall map they needed. "Here you go. The sanctuary is back that way. Bet they don't call it a sanctuary. That must be where those six escalators went. You said they have a service tonight?"

"Yep. 7:30 of the p.m."

"This is above and beyond, Bradford, but I think we need to go to it."

"I was afraid you might say that. But only if we stop at East Village Square on the way back to the station. *Real* malls have a Victoria's Secret."

They were staring at the map again. "We need the church offices. What's down this way?"

Bradford jabbed the glass with his finger. "That's WildLife 4 Youth Rampage. You don't want to go down there."

"It says they only rampage on Thursday nights. But we need to go the other way anyhow. Here are the offices. C'mon."

After about five more minutes of walking, they found the outer doors of the church office complex. They made their way in and were steered by some signage to the right, where the senior pastors' offices were. They walked across about half an acre of carpet that you could lose a croquet ball in, came to another set of glass doors, and went through those.

"Good morning. I'm Detective Rourke. This is Detective Bradford." Sharon Atwater stood up quickly, came around the desk, and shook both their hands.

"Good to meet both of you. I'll tell Chad you're here." She started off.

"No hurry, ma'am. We need to interview you too. Why don't we just start with that?"

Sharon felt something tighten in her throat. Her hand went up, and she quickly tucked her dark hair behind her right ear. "Chad was eager to visit with you. But we can do that. Please, have a seat."

"Is *Chad* Pastor Lester?" Bradford asked.

"Yes, yes. No formalities here at Camel Creek. Chad believes that a pastor must be approachable." *Wrong word. "Approaching" has all the wrong connotations. Call him Chad. When the conversation is filled with "Rev. Lesters," it must cool the adulterous vapors. At least in this denomination. Probably a turn-on in others. Focus, Sharon.* She sat down behind her desk and watched the detectives drag chairs over.

Bradford saw that she was nervous and tried to lighten the mood.

"That'll take some getting used to on my part. In my church back home, if I had ever called Pastor Hill *Bruce,* my mother would have found the dullest butter knife in her drawer and skinned me with it. Then she would have had the knife mounted as a trophy. No remorse on her part at all."

Sharon just stared at him. Tried to smile, but her cheek just twitched.

Rourke smiled grimly. "Thank you, Detective Bradford, for sharing that with us. My partner, Miss Atwater, has a slight touch of autism. Now if you don't mind . . ."

"My son was autistic." She didn't know why she was talking. She wanted to stop talking. No one at the church even knew she'd had a son. "I gave him up for adoption."

The detectives were looking at her. Rourke was trying to look sympathetic. Bradford was gaping.

Shut up, Sharon. Why am I talking like this? "I was in high school. I wouldn't give him up now. Not that I would have had him now. I wasn't in the fold in high school. I'm not married." She gripped herself firmly, forced her mouth shut, and looked away from the detectives. They were like priests to a long-lapsed and desperate Catholic. She stared at her computer. And there, her only comfort in life and in death, was the monitor wallpaper about a free milkshake given to God.

"I'm not really autistic," Bradford said.

"I know," she said.

"Um," Rourke cleared his throat. "Sorry about that, ma'am. I didn't mean any insensitivity."

"No, of course not. That's fine." She even laughed. "I don't really know why that came out." She laughed again. "Go ahead with your questions. I'll try not to drag my life story in again."

The next fifteen minutes were predictable and routine, as such interviews go. How long have you worked here? *Eleven years.* Have you had the same job since you were hired? *Yes.* Did you worship in this church before you were hired? *Yes.* How long? *About a year, maybe a little more.*

But at some point Robert P. Warner II slowly crept into the conversation. Sharon did not share Chad's gift for making panic invisible, and she was talking to detectives. They probably knew everything already. She would not be caught in a lie. They weren't asking questions that needed lies. *Do not tell a lie. Nobody is asking you to. There is no guilt here. You do not need to feel guilt. Answer the questions and then stop talking.* But despite her good advice to herself, she began to share far more than she had intended. Rourke was watching her hands and eyes, watching her hair get tucked behind her ears, watching her stare at her feet only to make herself look up at him and then glance away to that woman with the milkshake on her computer screen. Rourke's eyebrows went up, and his vast nautical experience taught him to expect a little plain sailing ahead. He jotted a note to Bradford, "Let her talk, let me ask." She never even looked at Bradford.

Sharon was thinking furiously. *Two more years. Back to Tennessee. Didn't sleep at all. Don't want to go to prison, especially not for Chad. What to do? What is this interview? Do I need an attorney? If I say anything about an attorney, do I look guilty of something? Not for* Chad. *But there is no guilt here. Plenty elsewhere, but not here.*

Sharon may have been visibly nervous, and her confidence was rattled, but still, her secretarial competence had been running on all eight cylinders before the detectives got there. She had a packet waiting for them.

"The paper said that Robert P. Warner claimed these incidents occurred ten years ago. That was one year after I came here, and I was the one who set up our current system of counseling logs. Here is the log for that year, and here are copies of the logs for the times when Warner claimed he was here. I can give you these because nothing in them pertains to what the people were seeing Chad about. Just the names and dates are here." Sharon's eye fell on the name Suzanne Perkins as she handed the copies across. *I remember her. Good thing the logs don't say anything about having bazooms fondled.* She looked back at her computer trying not to look like she was thinking about anything. *That woman got her free milkshake. Came out of there with her blouse buttoned very differently than when she went in.* As *she recalled. Funny. The milkshake lady looked a lot like Suzanne Perkins.*

Sharon stopped. Rourke wasn't looking at the packet. He just sat, quietly watching her, and so she resumed. "And so I think Warner's claims are simply not credible. He simply wasn't there at those times." Rourke knew that she had something else to say, and would say it if she had to. So he leaned forward in his seat, and started a very fruitful exchange in the realm of thought.

Do I have to? she wondered.

Do you know anything? It depends. It was a simple reply.

But I really don't think it's relevant.

But perhaps we should judge that, Rourke thought in return.

I don't want to get into trouble. Not worth it. Not for Chad.

We are not on a crusade. You can trust us.

Rourke really liked how this telepathic exchange was going. No messy paperwork.

"There is one more thing. But please . . ."

"Go on."

"I really don't think there is anything to this Warner. I don't know what got into him. But there have been, from time to time, a few heterosexual . . . missteps." *Is that enough?*

Not *quite* enough. "How are you sure?"

"Well, let's just say that a secretary sees and hears a lot. If Warner were a woman, I would have a hard time disbelieving the story. But as it is . . ." *That enough? You see? I was cooperative from the very first.*

Rourke nodded, satisfied, so Bradford did too. "I will try to keep it there."

"Thank you." *Thank you, thank you.* "Do you want to see Chad now?"

Rourke nodded again. *Make a note to tell Bradford. Always talk to the secretary first. You learn more about the boss from the secretary than you do from the boss about the secretary.*

Sharon walked down a hallway leading off from the reception area, put her head in at a door they couldn't see, and then came back. "Chad is ready to see you."

While this conversation was going on in the outer office, Chad had been sitting magisterially behind his desk, but nobody was looking. Doesn't hurt to practice. Why were they taking so long with Sharon? Erica had been a disappointment too. Very unresponsive. All she wanted to do was talk about the newspapers. Appreciated a pastor who remembered her needs and problems in the midst of his own. Made him late.

The two detectives walked in. "Detective Rourke. Detective Bradford," Sharon said.

Chad stood up and came around the desk, hand extended. "Please, call me Chad," he said heartily.

Bradford winced, but Rourke jumped right in. "Pleased to meet you, Chad."

Sharon was backing toward the door. "May I bring you all something to drink? Soda?"

"Yes, please, Sharon," Chad said. "Detective Rourke?"

"7-Up, please."

"Detective Bradford?"

"Diet brown something. Thanks."

"And I'll have my usual water. Thanks so much, Sharon."

After they were settled, drinks in hand, Rourke cleared his throat. "Chad, as the newspaper article made clear, Robert Warner has filed a civil suit against you and against the church. This is not a criminal case at all. At the same time, the allegations have caught the prosecutor's attention, and he wanted us to interview you at least once for our files." Rourke stopped to take a drink and mused thoughtfully to himself as he did so. The newspapers will be filled with Warner, Warner, Warner. The public already knows how to spell Warner. They need to know how to spell Radavic.

Chad nodded. "Go on."

"You are not a suspect in any criminal case, or even a person of interest. We just want to ask a few questions. Nevertheless, if you want to have an attorney present, that is certainly your right . . ."

Chad waved his hand dismissively. He had already talked to the attorneys, and they had gone over what he should and should not say. They thought it was best for him to talk with the cops without them, for at this stage of the proceedings, what could be better than nonchalance? And besides, they knew that Chad was good. *Nobody* slipperier. If the investigation turned serious, or turned into a real investigation somehow, the attorneys would then cluster round. "Right now," said Smith, the youngest attorney, "this is just to get Radavic into the papers. Our worry is the civil suit."

The same fifteen minutes were spent gathering background data, and the first speed bump came at, "Married?"

"Yes, for eighteen years. But unfortunately, the divorce is almost final."

"Sorry to hear that. Reasons?"

"Grew apart. Still the best of friends, though."

"Children?"

"Two lovely girls, Kimberly and Shannon. Still in high school."

"Robert P. Warner II?"

"Ah, here is where our interview has to end, but not because I want to be uncooperative. I know absolutely nothing about the man. Sharon has given you the logs. I am unable to help you. But I would help if I could."

Chad smiled a sad, pastoral smile. Rourke looked at him, sympathetically impressed. Man, this guy was good. But Rourke had been on the force for many years, and he was just as good. Rourke tightened the muscles in his jaw. That man across the desk is telling the truth for now, just this moment. But he is a liar telling the truth, and it almost suits him.

So Rourke just sat and watched admiringly. Chad chose his words with care, but with a carefree care. Everything was parsed, but looked as though it was spontaneously lying about. Shabby chic.

". . . obviously a troubled young man, and I would help him if I could. For anyone to abuse a pastoral relation with a young man that way . . ." Rourke noted the effortless way in which Chad denounced pastoral abuse—with young men. Everything positioned just so. Everything anticipated. Plausible deniability in every direction.

The detectives rose to go. Thanks so much. Anytime. At your disposal. We want this resolved as fast as possible. Can you direct us to Miguel Smith's office? That way, then left. Morning. Morning. Enjoy the sun. Thanks again. Sure. Bye.

/ / / / / /

Miguel Smith, unlike virtually everyone else at Camel Creek, had blue-collar roots and blue-collar sensitivities. He had worked the orchards as a young man, knew what calluses were, and did not put on affectations. Got his CPA in night classes and was, taking one thing with another, an industrious and robust character, belonging to the classic Long John Silver school of thought. Enrolled in the curriculum of the seven deadlies, he almost entirely bypassed sloth, but had a double major in avarice and lust. His gruff manner had all the bookkeepers cowed and was one of the reasons he had such an easy time keeping a second set of books. It was a sweet setup. He had the sweetest setup in the history of the world, short of a few popes. No shareholders. No product. No inventory.

Every separate collection was counted with three deacons in the room at all times, and was counted three times. At Miguel's insistence, the procedures were established so that each deacon had to sign a paper verifying the amount on the deposit slip, and the bag and deposit slip were then left with Miguel. He would take 10 percent off the top, fill out a new deposit slip—instead of the previous separate ones, amazed that nobody appeared to know what he was doing—and would report to the elders and deacons the combined totals for all the services every weekend. Because he only reported the combined totals, and because there was such a show of hyperaccountability in the procedures, everyone thought they were setting new standards in the levels of accountability.

He had started the operation at 2 percent, but it worked so well that he inched himself up to 10 percent, and there he settled. No point in being greedy. Since the deacons who signed their respective papers were only there for one service, and Miguel didn't break it out for them in the report, and the sum totals always *looked* close, and the remaining 90 percent that they did have was enormous, Miguel looked like a rock of integrity at its finest. If he had been more evangelical than he was, and if he had ever actually read the Bible for himself, he would have justified things to himself with that passage about an ox and a muzzle and treading grain. But he needed no justification because he felt no guilt. Good, strong personal finance. Tax-free.

The only one he hadn't been able to fool was Chad, who was more than happy to look the other way, so long as the hidden funds were available to help out the occasional fallen woman. "Miguel," he would say, "can you help me out with a troubled lady?"

Occasionally Miguel would whistle through his teeth and mention that hookers in nearby towns were cheaper, but at the same time, he was philosophical about it. Nearby towns would involve gas money.

"Morning. Detective Rourke. This is Detective Bradford."

"Good to meet you. Miguel Smith. How can I help you?"

"This is a question in the abstract. I am not asking for this now, but just wanted to know what would happen if I did ask. If we were to ask you if any money had ever been paid out to a Robert P. Warner, would you be able to tell us?"

"Well, boyo, it's like this. If you were to ask, and if you had a subpoena, we could get you that information in ten minutes. Without a subpoena, I can't tell you anything, though I might go so far as to say, 'Oink, oink, I smell bacon,' but only in the nicest way. With a subpoena, you could ask, and it would come up empty. Already ran the check. Sorry I can't give you any papers to that effect without a subpoena. But just so you know, you're yelling up the wrong rainspout. Warner has not received any money from Camel Creek. Not that he doesn't want to, mind. Come back in a year and I might be able to show you a big check made out to him. But that wouldn't help you gentlemen any."

The detectives thanked him for his help, and after the usual pleasantries, they made their way out again. On the top of the river rock stairs, facing the waiting parking lot, Rourke and Bradford just stood quietly for a few moments. Suddenly Rourke broke the silence.

"Bradford, as much as it troubles me to do this in front of you, I have to admit that I don't understand these people at all. You're already ahead of me with that radio station thing, and we both have to come to the service tonight. And maybe we should go back inside to the bookshop and buy ourselves a few bestsellers. A couple by the Rev. Lester might be helpful."

NEWS BABE

Nine times out of ten, the coarse word is the word that condemns an evil and the refined word the word that excuses it.

G. K. Chesterton

THE SUNSET WAS BEAUTIFULLY UNDERSTATED, and spread out over the western sky like the pale, pastel inside of an oyster shell. But it had been *quite* a day, and the oyster was a little annoyed. Sharon Atwater stood at the top of the stairs leading down to the parking lot, and looked out at the quiet evening, peeved. *She* was peeved, not the evening, although the evening was thinking about it. At the bottom of the stairs was a local television station truck, big satellite dish on the top, and cords running all over heck. Several cameras were already set up, and it looked like they were about to go live. *Car is right on the other side of that mess. I could walk through, but they might start asking me questions. Not for Chad.* Sharon swiveled and started to walk the long way around.

From a distance, she could see the two detectives who had visited her earlier getting out of the car they had just parked right behind hers. *Fantastic. They're waiting for me. Great. They found out I was lying and came to arrest me. But I wasn't lying. Not for Chad.* There was nothing to do but keep walking the long way around, so she did.

But the two policemen were not waiting for her. They were standing there for the same reason that Sharon was now going the long way around—the television crew. But they weren't moving, because they didn't know the long way around to the front doors. Rourke had an aggrieved look on his face.

"Why, Bradford, do I always have to deal with News Babe?"

Bradford didn't know. "Righteous living?"

Rourke shifted from one foot to the other, drumming his fingers on the roof of the car. "If we walk up the stairs, she will see us. And if she sees us, she will jump out at us, all blond and brassy like. And she will pepper us with questions. I don't want to talk to News Babe, Bradford."

"Maybe there is a long way around," Bradford said, and looking off to the left, saw Sharon Atwater approaching her car. "Well, look at this," he said.

Both detectives stood up straight, and greeted her cordially. "Evening, ma'am," Rourke said. "Is there a way around this televised blond pestilence? Without moving our car?"

Sharon, relieved beyond words, silently pointed to the walkway she had just come down, hidden artfully behind the junipers. They exchanged a few observations about the sunset and began to make their way around.

The detectives did not know the ropes at Camel Creek, and so they were almost a half an hour early for the service. This, in Camel Creek time, was an eternity and was why the parking lot was almost entirely empty. Most of the expert attendees knew how to shave it just right, surging into the meeting room just minutes before the action started, and skiing out immediately afterward, an hour and fifteen minutes later. Bradford and Rourke were there early enough to rattle around artlessly for aeons. If they had been there fifteen minutes earlier than *that*, they would have had time to join the band and practice several numbers.

They made it to the walkway at the top of the stairs and were headed toward the long row of doors, almost there, when one of the news crew, the main cameraman, spotted them. He turned to News Babe, and tugged at her sleeve. "Looky there," he said.

News Babe was strikingly good-looking. She was gorgeous. She was so good-looking that when she first started out in television five years before, everyone who saw her simply assumed that she was an idiot, and so she had determined early in her career that she would have to be *really* aggressive, journalistically imperious, dictatorial to her staff, and merciless to anyone who got between her and the story. And it had worked. Nobody thought she got her position by her looks anymore, because no one was really able to keep in mind the fact that she was beautiful anymore, except in that mandatory newsbaby kind of way.

Well, actually, Rourke's wife knew she was good-looking because her husband always called her News Babe. She didn't like it, but there it was. But he had explained a number of times that he was not lusting in his heart, and that she was his mortal enemy. She had no allure; she was charming in the same way that Tokyo Rose had been charming to her grandfather in the middle of the Pacific. She was to him as Moriarty had been to Sherlock, if Moriarty had been blonde, stacked, and pushy. Every high-profile case, there she was with the truck, getting underfoot like a toddler on a rainy day. "Hmmff," his wife sniffed. "Look at that blouse. *Three* buttons undone. The factory puts them on for a reason, you know."

News Babe was there with the cameras for two reasons. She was, first, on a constant lookout for stories that had the capacity to catapult a local area news reporter (like *her*, say) into the New York City big time. If anything had that "feel," as this story most certainly did, she was right there. Other reporters could have been assigned to this one, but News Babe had sharp elbows and she knew how to throw them.

The second reason was more personal, and a bit harder to file under zeal for professional advancement. About three years prior, she had been covering the ribbon-cutting ceremony for the Camel Creek crisis pregnancy center, and about fifteen minutes after the ceremony had officially wrapped up, she had chanced to overhear Chad Lester and Miguel Smith talking about—public figures really need to remember that microphones, even the little ones, are *always* on—her retreating figure. Smith had said, quite appreciatively, that she looked like a couple of bear cubs fighting in a small sack. Lester had replied, more dismissively, that she would do in a pinch. They both were speaking in a way that relied more on Anglo-Saxon vocabulary than church leaders ought to have been doing, and so News Babe knew that they were both hypocritical scoundrels. But that is not what rankled her—she had grown up in a youth group that had made her quite cynical on that score. It was the dismissiveness in Lester's comments that got to her. Her sense of propriety was not nearly so insulted as her vanity was. She might be able to get to New York *and* settle a score on the way out.

"Rourke!" News Babe shouted.

Ten feet away from the safety of the front doors, his shoulders drooped, and he turned wearily around. Bradford turned and stood with him, heroically.

She walked briskly up to them, her blouse bouncing provocatively, as much as to say in stereo that we *dare* you to do anything but look at our forehead. She had a small microphone and tape recorder in a bag over her shoulder. "May I ask you a few questions?"

"Certainly," Rourke said.

"Why are you here?"

"Worshipping," Bradford said.

News Babe turned a baleful eye on him.

"Don't mind my colleague," Rourke said. "We are here for the same reason you are, and we don't have anything to share with you just yet. If we ever do, I am sure you will be the first with the story."

"Is that a promise, Rourke?"

More like *fate*, he thought. "Promise," he said.

They turned back to the front doors, and when they were inside, Rourke said to Bradford, "And if that happens, *you're* doing the interview. You're young. Your marriage is resilient."

The two men rode silently and alone up the seven escalators. A few official-looking people with electronic thingies hanging off them were scurrying around the lobby area at the top of the escalators, but the congregation was yet to arrive. Outside the doors of the auditorium, they could hear the slapping and thumping of a hopping bass line, and opened the doors just as the rehearsed number had the plug kicked out of it.

"No, no, three measures in. Then *hit* it." The worship leader with a head set on was gesturing at one of the guitar players.

"Got it," the guitar player said.

Bradford looked around him, and as the King James Version he read while growing up would have put it, he was *astonied*. The auditorium was like a gigantic version of a college classroom, only there were cushioned theater seats there for ten thousand. The seats were in a huge semicircle, in two tiers. In between the tiers was an open sound booth that looked like it had about fifteen sound engineers in it. Two giant screens were hanging on either side of the stage, ready for a multimedia presentation. The band was in the middle, and a stool sat off to the side for the pastor.

They were about halfway down the tier closest to the stage, and both stood there, disoriented. But newcomers *always* came early, and so an usher was there to greet them inside a minute. "It's great to serve the King," he said. "First time here?" he asked.

They both nodded, and he showed them to a nearby seat and gave them both a program.

"A program?" Rourke asked.

"We do worship differently here," the young man grinned.

They sat down and tried to kill some time reading over the program. But as programs go, this one was in the minimalist school. Just enough information to make sure people could always figure out how much time was left, and not enough to figure out what was actually going on. The program had five words on it—worship, clips, worship, share, and reachout. But if "reachout" is actually two words, that would affect the total count, making it six words.

But there was more to read on the back of the program. There was a place to fill out name and e-mail address, along with boxes to check next to any felt needs that the visitor might have that the trained readers of the checked boxes might be able to help the visitor with. Underneath the blank for the name was the word *optional*. Bradford brightened when he saw that, and got out his pen. "I bet we will learn a lot about their approach to sinners this way," he said, and began to check boxes. When he was done, he handed it to Rourke, who looked it over solemnly.

"They are going to think you are one screwed up puppy," he said finally.

"Yes, but they will have no choice but to send me their information, in all the following areas. And the beauty of it is I don't have to give my name. All I have to do is create a new e-mail account when I get home."

"Turdinthepunchbowl@hotmail.com."

"*Exactly.* They will think I have low self-esteem and will be very kind to me."

"You checked the boxes next to bulimia, obesity, porn addiction, sex addiction, dysfunctional family, marriage counseling, anger management, and substance abuse."

"Yes, but it is not *true.* This is kind of like undercover work."

While they had been talking, the auditorium was filling up, efficiently and quietly. Promptly at five minutes before the time of the service, the band broke into a hot little jam, no vocals. People began taking their seats, and the detectives looked around curiously. It was a midweek service, and so the upper tier, behind the sound booth, was empty. The lower tier, however, was almost full.

At 7:30, on the dot, the lights went down, and the words of a song flashed up on both screens. The band moved seamlessly from their jam into the new song, as tight as a backup band for Springsteen on a good night. The assembled congregants began to sing, or so the two men guessed from the fact that words were on the screen, and people's mouths were moving, but the amplified music from up front had all of them buried. Bradford had been to one or two concerts like this in his life before, but Rourke felt like he was under an acoustical rock pile.

There was no break between songs, each one moving aside when its time was done, and allowing another to merge flawlessly to take its place. The whole thing was like a superbly engineered six-lane highway with two lanes merging from the right. But after four songs, the screens suddenly changed, and the band fell suddenly silent. A montage of clips from news shows, sitcoms, and movies suddenly filled the screens on the next beat, and the voice-over began to ask a series of penetrating questions. "What are we to make of the postmodern anguish? How can the church address it if the church refuses to hear the postmodern voice—raw, uncensored, honest, full of integrity? When will *we* share that integrity and partner with it?"

After ten minutes of clips, the music jumped in again, and Rourke found he was actually getting used to it. But this second segment was made up of top-40 songs, which meant that Bradford knew some of the words. It also meant that the church was listening to some raw postmodern anguish, full of integrity, which seemed to be mostly about boyfriends who don't call anymore. But after fifteen minutes of *that*, the time that the program had called *share* came up.

A spotlight fell suddenly on the stool they had seen earlier, and both detectives were startled to see Chad Lester sitting there. Martin had been slated to do the midweek, which Chad almost never did anymore, but a decision had been made earlier that day that because of the scandal, Chad should get out there in front. Show of confidence. No blood in the water *here*.

"Speaking of partnering with integrity . . ." Bradford whispered.

The two policemen had thought Lester was smooth when they were talking with him in his office earlier that day. But *now*—his voice was mellifluous and constant. Whenever he paused, always at just the right moment, sincerity oozed out of the silences and puddled on the floor. He sat on the stool easily, at peace with God and man. His hair, gray in all the appropriate places, bespoke experience and accumulated wisdom. His blue polo shirt was gracefully unbuttoned at the neck, and his slacks were as crisp as they come. He hit his consonants perfectly, and the vowels did not betray his regional origins.

"When we speak of the emergent church, leaving certain things behind, we are only rejecting that which is tired and worn out. We retain the best that our fathers have left for us, and we retain it with gratitude. But we are still resolved to meet the challenges of the contemporary world around us, and to enter into a truly creative dialogue with it. And this is where we must learn a little humility . . . for dialogue will not be *truly* creative if we are not willing to listen and learn from what our discussion partners have to say. Why should the church not learn from some of the best secular thinkers today on the best positions for women in the church, for example?"

The two men were not swayed, but they were agape at this talent on display. But when Chad got to that unfortunate phrase "positions for women," the spell was broken for both detectives. Each of them suddenly had unsavory questions arise in their minds about what *other* meanings Chad might be entertaining for the phrase "best positions for women," which, had Chad been thinking, would have been "the position *of* women." And those unsavory questions involved things that had nothing to do with equality, dignity, or acceptable public summaries. The moment of resumed clarity was, for the detectives, not unlike that time when Wormtongue pitched the Palantir off the tower of Orthanc.

Chad was good, really good, no question. But Chad was also on cruise control. The panic he had felt earlier in the day was still romping around inside him, still robust, and still showing no signs of coming down off its manic high. Not only did he have a panic party going on down there, but it was a bipolar panic party on the upside of things and no meds in sight. Chad had noticed the trouble phrase "best positions for women" too, and if he had not been so distracted, he never would have said anything like that, especially in the middle of a *sex* scandal. Of course, the fact that the scandal was all about a bimbo named Robert meant that it was probably okay. But still, focus, focus. Guys aren't bimbos. What would that be, anyway? Bimbus?

At the same time, spectacularly, on top of his flailing and increasingly rambunctious panic below, the flow of words continued smoothly, effortlessly, cogently, compellingly.

"The emergent church today poses a threat to powerful interests in our day, interests who know how to *retaliate.*"

This was his one reference to the scandal, understood instantly by everyone in the auditorium. Understated perfectly. No self-pity here. Shrewd insight. Political savvy. Courage. The tennis ball right in the sweet spot. *Angela plays tennis. Angela lives right next to the country club. You are free-associating, Chad. You have a talk to finish.* Which he did, right on the money.

The band kicked in perfectly, and the reachout postlude jam began the same moment that the spotlight on Chad's stool cut off. The two detectives stood up and stretched. Everyone else was standing, and it appeared the accepted protocol was to visit for just a moment and then head for the escalators. Bradford dropped his program in a box designated for "felt needs requests," and they rode down the escalators without speaking.

They sat in the parking lot for about ten minutes, waiting to get out. Bradford found KING on the radio, which they were both listening to absently. "You said you didn't understand these people, boss. How about now?" In reply, Rourke made a strange, whistling sound in his teeth. When they finally made it up to the feeder road that would take them down to the interstate, Chad's small red Ferrari came from around the back of the church, buzzed in front of them along that feeder road, and headed off to Angela's.

SOME NORMAL PEOPLE

The devil's boots don't creak.
Scottish proverb

Pastor mitchell was leaning back in his chair, feet on his desk, phone balanced on his shoulder. "Uh huh," he was saying. And occasionally he said, "Go on." The church was small, and therefore his study was at home, and this is what accounted for his wife appearing suddenly in the doorway.

"Just a sec," he said to the person on the other end. "What? . . . Okay, call me later." He hit the talk button and wondered briefly why he had to push the talk button when the call was over and he was done talking, but then put the receiver on top of a stack of commentaries that enlarged at great length on St. Paul's second extant letter to the Corinthians.

"I am picking Sandy up after her rehearsal, and then we are hitting Costco. We will be home before dinner, but if the oven beeps, you should be able to hear it in here."

"I hate it when you leave me."

"You're a dear and a love. But would you get the casserole out if you hear the beeping? Thanks bunches, sweetie. And since that is your sole responsibility for the next hour, you should be able to do exegesis like crazy. Or whatever it is you do in here."

"I hate it when you leave me."

Cindi stuck her head back in. "Did you see the paper this morning? About Camel Creek?"

"No, but that was George on the phone just now. I got the lowdown."

"What are we going to do about Cherie?" Cherie was Cindi's cousin and had been at Camel Creek forever. Being an attractive woman and one who had been at Camel Creek forever, some years earlier she had, not surprisingly, been the recipient of some of the Rev. Lester's more earthy ministrations. Despite this, or perhaps because of it, she was doggedly loyal to the humidity levels of Camel Creek, and would have nothing to do with the high mountain air of Grace Reformed, the church where Mitchell was pastor.

John muttered to himself, and then answered, "I could call her up and invite her to church *here.* And she would certainly think, and perhaps say, that she was grateful for the invitation, but *she* prefers to worship where people love each other. I think I'll pass."

"*I'll* say they love each other." Cindi was then down the hall and out the door.

Grace Reformed was a small Reformed Baptist church, and Pastor Mitchell had been there for twelve years, which was something of a record for Reformed Baptist churches in that region. The previous three pastors had been there for about a year and a half each, and the last of the three had been the kind of fellow who typed long doctrinal screeds to errant fellow ministers, single-spaced, and with typing up the sides of the margins. Some thought that he had mastered the art of typing with his fists, and sometimes with his knees. Anyhow, his pulpit ministrations had left the congregation in an exhausted frame of mind, and parishioners would go home after the message, recline on the sofa, and pant. The sermons were of the "all grace, no slack" variety, and more than a few worshippers were concerned about just how much more grace their families could take. But after the last of these three gentleman imploded one Sunday in the pulpit, trying to fit infinite predestination into his thimblebrain and from thence into the sermon, the search committee decided to try something a little different, and went on the recommendation of a parishioner's cousin instead of the recommendation of the bishop. Now, Baptists don't have bishops—at least not that anybody admits to—but at any rate, the bishop was very angry and Grace Reformed was drummed out of the elite corps of regional churches.

But according to one old-timer in the church, Pastor John Mitchell himself had been like "a balm in Gibeah, or maybe it is Gilead. Something with a G, but not Gotham." At any rate, the congregation perked up again like a sun-fried plant that somebody left on a deck with full southern exposure while the family went on vacation for two weeks in August, and which an unexpected someone decided to water at just the right time and in the right amounts when they got back. It was like a miracle. The slow bleed of families away from the church was stopped, the church stabilized for a number of years, and just in the last six months three new families had joined. In Grace Reformed terms, this was considered a massive revival, and everybody was more than content. Pastor Mitchell had been in 2 Corinthians for two years now and was only in chapter seven. This, compared to his predecessors, made him a speed demon, and the only reason he was going as slowly as this was that he kept getting distracted by pastoral needs, and he kept turning aside to use the text to encourage people.

This was a novelty, and given the history of the church, he might not have been able to get away with it, had his personal appearance not been just right, providing a certain amount of camouflage. He was a regular Tishbite—gray beard, bushy eyebrows, and slender build. And though he didn't eat locusts or wild honey all that much, he still managed to look like a cross between Moses, Elijah, John the Baptist, and Gandalf. But for all that he was only forty-two and very spry. He did not take a staff with him into the pulpit, but all younger children in the church felt like he must have an invisible one up there with him. The kids were regularly on the edge of their pews, Sunday after Sunday, waiting for him to part the waters of the baptistery in the middle of a sermon. He looked severe enough that no one really noticed that he was not severe at all, and this meant that no one had a conscience attack or felt like they were going soft in their Calvinism because he always *looked* like he was being strict with them. So things were swell at Grace Reformed.

Pastor Mitchell reached for one of the commentaries and twaddled it back and forth for a moment. But then he put it down and reached for the phone again. One of the visitors that they had intermittently had over the past year was an old college roommate of Mitchell's, a stockbroker named Brian Lewis. He was not a member, or even what you would call a believer, but he came to worship semiregularly, and the two men got along well enough. Pastor Mitchell remembered that Brian had told him about six months ago that he was "seeing" Chad Lester's wife. Brian had shuffled and scraped his feet in the parking lot while they had talked about it, and he had done so in such an industrious manner that it suggested he was studying a new dance step. "They are going to be divorced anyhow, the guy's a real toad; all over but the paperwork." Pastor Mitchell had been looking for an opportunity to talk with him further about things, and this appeared to be it.

He looked up the number of Brian's brokerage firm and punched the buttons pastorally, the quiet beep-booping filling the study.

"Brian? John. Hey, I've been meaning to talk to you about Mrs. Lester, and what with the blowup over at Camel Creek today, I thought that maybe we should get together. You still seeing her?"

John Mitchell sat quietly for the next ten minutes as a torrent of information flowed over him. Finally, when the flow had subsided to about knee high, he decided to attempt wading upstream a little bit. "So this is really a theological problem for you?"

An excited murmuring came over the line.

"I mean that you believe that Chad Lester is guilty of every sexual offense a man can be guilty of, except for the one he is actually accused of, and it makes you wonder if there is any justice in the world or, if there is justice, whether it is dabbling too much in literary ironies."

Something like a strangled shout came over the line.

"Okay, okay. Want to get together for lunch? Friday? Great . . . fine. We should go somewhere that is an unlikely place for any of the elders of Camel Creek to be . . . no, not Hooters. And I was joking anyhow."

When the time and place were set, and Brian expressed his thanks multiple times—he *really* wanted to talk to somebody— John hung up the phone. He rocked back in his chair and stared thoughtfully at the picture of his family on the opposite wall, just above the sofa covered with multiple stacks of books, all of them written by men with fifty-pound heads. Most of them were now deceased, and John used to declare from the pulpit that being dead had done nothing but *add* to their orthodoxy. For her part, Cindi had often told him that *he* was the theological equivalent of a mad scientist and had added the corollary that sofas were for sitting on.

John Mitchell had only met Chad Lester twice. The first time had been at the governor's prayer breakfast, and the meeting had been brief and cordial. John was new in town at the time, had not a clue, and was prepared to be friends with everybody. But the second time was about five years later, after he and

Cindi had walked cousin Cherie—who was alternatively clingy with and hostile to her helpful relatives—through and around the emotional crater left after her three-day affair with the pastor. The ministerial luncheon was just two weeks after Cherie's grand meltdown, and John had only barely been able to contain his desire to extend the right hand of fellowship to Chad's left ear, and to do so in a less-than-tender fashion. But he had resisted the temptation manfully, and had walked away from *that* encounter with the devil as a tested and nobler soul. At least that is what he told Cindi for about three weeks afterward, at the end of which time she told him he'd lost almost all his treasure in heaven about two and a half weeks before. "You were doing good right at the start," she said. "But then you *noticed* how good you were doing. But you're my sweet baby anyway," she said.

His reverie was finally interrupted by a distant sound, the significance of which John thought he might know. What was that? It sounded like somebody was punching buttons on the phone with a monotonous regularity. What could that be? After a couple of minutes in communion with what appeared to be a real puzzler, John jolted in his chair. The *oven!* He jumped down the hall and slid into the kitchen the way he always did when nobody was home. He wasn't sure that the apostle Paul would do something like that, but there was no clear prohibition of it anywhere. And besides, his socks were slippy.

The surface of the casserole was nicely brown, just the way he liked, and he put the oven mitts back in the drawer, highly pleased with himself. He was getting a drink out of the fridge, since he was there, when the door from the garage opened and Sandy bounced in, followed by Cindi.

"Hi, Daddy," Sandy said, and kissed him on the cheek.

Cindi looked at the casserole on the counter, and said, "Way to go, champ."

"I hovered over it the whole time," he said.

"Pastors shouldn't tell such dreadful lies," Sandy said.

"I know. I'm trying to taper off. How was Costco?"

"A perfect madhouse," Cindi said. "Sandy, tell your dad what you heard at school."

"Oh!" Sandy said, and paused to collect herself, in order to present the story as she thought it deserved to be presented. There was nothing particularly different about this story—she did the same thing every night, with *all* her stories.

"You know that Trey is in my class? Well, Trey is friends with the Lester girls, and in homeroom, when Mrs. Jordan was taking prayer requests, he said that they said the accusations against their dad couldn't be right because Robert P. Warner, that's the guy in the newspaper, was living with a woman named Mystic Union."

"I am not sure I'm following the argument," Pastor Mitchell said. "Was it an argument?"

"Oh, I don't know that—I don't know what they were saying, or how much Trey was messing it up."

"And Mrs. Jordan let Trey say all that?"

"She was trying to stop him. And Ryan—Ryan from our church—was yelling, 'Overshare! Overshare!' from the back of the room."

"So why should I be interested in this? Help me out here."

Sandy laughed. "Don't you remember who Mystic Union is?"

John Mitchell stood in the middle of the kitchen floor, scratching his beard. Suddenly his eyes widened. "Mrs. Winmore!"

Pastor Winmore had been the pastor of Grace Reformed prior to John, the one who blew up one day in the middle of Romans 9—an easy thing to do, admittedly—and after he had been committed to the state hospital, she stayed in the congregation for about six months, although she was only present for about three months of John Mitchell's initial tenure there. She had been a very quiet woman, but one day she apparently decided to go on an epistemological bender. She had grown up Dutch Reformed, become a Reformed Baptist at Bible school, and had married the Rev. Winmore as a consequence of this, or perhaps the other way around, and then had settled into the stereotypical role of a pastor's wife. She was a strikingly handsome woman, with shoulder-length black and gray hair, but it was not the kind of gray hair that was wispy and stuff, but rather thick and full and long and rich. She looked like a boomer lady in a television commercial for osteoporosis medicine, the kind of lady who did not really need the medicine, but who might look as though some day soon she *could*.

One day something snapped, like a dry twig in one of Fenimore Cooper's novels, and after she divorced Pastor Winmore, off she went to a healing school specializing in naturopathy, herbs, channeling, and other forms of New Age hooey. She had transferred her membership to Camel Creek, but only as an intermediate step to founding her own idea of a Buddhist temple in the back of a storefront in the older part of town. She changed her name to Mystic Union and became exceedingly garrulous, up to and including occasional radio spots advertising her herbal remedies. She had been really quiet for all her years as a pastor's wife because she was one of those rare individuals whose wise and sagacious appearance was immediately contradicted as soon as she opened her mouth. In conservative Christian circles this necessitated a certain wariness in speaking, as a few unfortunate incidents at Bible studies had made clear, but she had now suddenly veered into a setting that made all such discretion most unnecessary.

"So, Mystic Union is living with Robert P. Accuser Guy?"

"According to the Lester girls, according to Trey, with Mrs. Jordan vainly trying to get her foot on the brake," Sandy said.

John Mitchell began to feel like something hot and wet was crawling up his spine. An hour and a half ago, the events at Camel Creek had seemed to him like an event on the local news horizon, which at sea is about eight miles away. That is, the events may have been interesting, but were certainly something that could be ignored when it came time for him to get on with the affairs of his life. But *then,* within that aforesaid hour and a half, three separate points of personal connection had started yelling at him, trying to get his attention. There was Cherie. There was always Cherie. There was Brian Lewis, attending Grace Reformed pretty regularly now, and he was dating the wife of Chad Lester. And now here was the ex-wife of *his* predecessor, living together with the accuser of Camel Creek's resident holy man. John had learned years before that there are no coincidences in pastoral ministry. He had learned to read the story. If the author has a character put a shotgun next to the mantelpiece in chapter 3, you can expect to see that shotgun later on in the book. John felt he had better keep an eye on that shotgun. This was beginning to feel like a setup. John began to look suspiciously around the kitchen.

"What do you want?" Cindi asked him. "I'll get it for you."

"I want," John said darkly, "*answers.*"

"You're the pastor," Sandy said brightly. "I bet *those* are back in your study."

Pastor Mitchell cleared his throat, and *humphed* back down the hall.

"Ten minutes!" his wife called after him.

HARMONIC CONVERGENCE

You cannot successfully determine beforehand
which side of the bread to butter.
Mrs. Murphy's Corollary

THE MORNING AFTER their sortie to the Camel Creek midweek service, Bradford and Rourke decided that they should try to interview Robert P. Warner "his own self," as Bradford put it. They asked around and got the address and contact info, and also discovered the existence of Mystic Union, a person mentioned in the newspaper article, albeit obliquely. Rourke hung up the phone after talking with one of the newspaper reporters.

"She told me Mystic Union is a real piece of work. Try to imagine Miss Boulder, Colorado, on steroids. And we will have to go through her if we want to talk with ol' Robert."

Bradford nodded and looked down at the piece of paper Rourke handed him. "1515 Asbury. I know where that is. Just on the genteel side of seedy. Safe but not savory."

Rourke snorted. "You used to work as a tour guide that side of town?"

"I am not saying I did or I didn't. But if I did, would that be so bad? Suppose a college student needed pizza money, say."

The two detectives stood up, stretched, and headed out to their car.

As it happened, Pastor Mitchell was heading for the same place. He was driving into town from the other direction, listening to the car radio more carefully than usual. He almost never listened to KING because "it got him out of fellowship," as he put it, but he was doing so this morning to see if there would be any references to the scandal at all. He had decided this morning, somewhat abruptly, that he needed to contact Mrs. Winmore, a.k.a. Mystic Union, before his lunch appointment with Brian. His pastoral antennae were buzzing and sparking, and it seemed to him that he was inevitably going to be dragged into this swamp of charges and countercharges. And if so, he preferred going in headfirst and not grabbed at the heels by the swamp monster of circumstances in order to be dragged helplessly into these stagnant ponds of punk water. He was just doing his duty, but his duty seemed a lot bigger than normal.

He was going to be talking to Cherie *regardless,* he was seeing Brian tomorrow, and he had kind of a historical connection to Mrs. Winmore. So on the drive into town he was trying to think of some plausible way he could phrase the question he *did* have for her, but the real reason for going was simply to make face-to-face contact with her again. Just in case. Just in case something happened that required him to be involved.

/ / / / / /

In that very same town, a man named Charles Peaborne had been up all night, getting his website ready to launch—a website that displayed at least some measure of historical literacy by its domain name of savonarola.com. Up until yesterday, Peaborne had been a deputy assistant to Miguel Smith, the roving Caribbean pirate of Camel Creek, and had been serenely unconscious of all the goings-on around him for many years. This was not unlike a first mate to Blackbeard believing himself to actually have been assistant to Florence Nightingale, but Peaborne was the kind of man who was entirely up to this kind of challenge. He was a classic paper-clip counter, correct-department-code-numbers-for-the-copying-machine maintainer, and one who generally focused on pennies, policies, and those blank "spirit of the law" spaces in between the lines of all written procedures—but only so long as "spirit of the law" was interpreted and applied by a committee of first-century Talmudic scholars, all of whom who had the disposition of a caged cinnamon bear with a sore head. Somewhat surly, in other words, in a passive-aggressive, muted sort of way.

At a department meeting just the previous week, Peaborne had pitched a fit over the use of a particularly expensive grade of paper in the annual reports, and had warned ominously that continued prodigality like this would be sure to bring down the wrath of heaven on *all* the ministries of Camel Creek. And of course, when the scandal erupted, he considered himself to have been fully vindicated in every way, not only on the question of the grade of paper for the annual reports, but also on the very similar warnings he had issued over the years concerning other matters of extravagance, not to mention the matters where people had the temerity to disagree with him.

He had turned in his ultimatum letter to Miguel with a stiff and censorious formality, a posture well-practiced, and after he was fired, had then gone home to create a web page that would tear the lid off Camel Creek and all its nefarious doings. In short, he was a very sore and fanatically gnat-strangling ex-employee, and he had three months of unemployment coming in which he might be able to settle at least a few scores. All his scruples were wound tight around his axle, and the more he gunned the engine, the more things were starting to smoke deep inside his head. He had that rare ability, nonexistent in the physical world, to read the teeny bottom line at the bottom of the optometrist's eye chart at fifty yards, but could not make out that big E thing at the top while standing next to it. He was the same man who had signed *all* the checks payable to former occupants of Chad Lester's rotating seraglio, a datum arranged with foresighted glee on Miguel's part, and one that would come back to render Charles more or less speechless later.

His new website catalogued the many evil decisions of Camel Creek staff over the years, the first of which was the toner cartridge debacle, and in a moment of inspiration at the last minute, he had decided to put some links off to the side—"What *Others* Are Saying About Camel Creek"—and he thought that perhaps he could get Robert P. Warner to provide him with a zingy quotation or two. So before getting some much needed sleep, he decided to drive downtown in search of Robert P. also. He got the address by googling around a bit and discovered in the process that Robert, in addition to his prowess in allegations of wrongdoing when it came to inappropriate touching by pastors, was also a true pasty blogger poet with greasy brown hair hanging in the eyes just *right,* and a sleepy look that suggested profundity more than bewilderment. Which just goes to show. Robert P. was something of a prophet also, with themes of High Apocalypse, shrill leftism, a goodish bit of principled narcissism, and some touches of Mormon theology in there somewhere.

And so thus it was that Bradford and Rourke came around one corner at exactly the same moment that Pastor Mitchell came around the other corner, and Charles Peaborne was walking across the street. They were all walking toward the front doors of the Health Temple, which meant also that they were all walking toward a satellite news truck with News Babe standing on the sidewalk in front. The Health Temple used to be a hardware store, and was spacious and wide across the front—it was built back in the thirties when linear dirt along the street was cheap. It was a brick building in good repair, and the white paint on the brick had just been applied the summer before last. A small tattoo parlor was off to the right side, just next door, and two doors down on the left was a barbeque chicken joint, which was the real reason for Bradford's knowledge of the area. "They make it just like this place in Memphis that I used to go to all the time," is what Bradford would have said had he been asked, but he wasn't.

Charles Peaborne was closest, but since he was coming from behind the satellite truck from across the street, News Babe didn't see him at all. She had turned to face Pastor Mitchell, and Peaborne scooted right behind her and in through the front door. Bradford and Rourke got safely past also, but paused sympathetically with their hands on the door handles, waiting to see how Pastor Mitchell, whom they did not know at all, but empathized with as a fellow human being, would fare. What they saw encouraged them both greatly, and later proved to be the beginning of the basis for a long-standing friendship with the stalwart man of God.

Microphone brandished at the appropriate angle, News Babe stepped forward and asked,

"Are you a customer of the Health Temple?"

"No, ma'am."

News Babe was not really doing customer interviews anyhow and was checking her recording levels more than anything, although she (from force of habit) was also conducting something of a fishing expedition in the questions she chose.

"Are you the co-owner, Robert P. Warner?"

"No, ma'am."

Pastor Mitchell was looking at News Babe through narrow slits, mostly because the morning sun was right in his eyes, but also because he thought it was the only appropriate way to talk with this woman. He used to see her regularly on television, but about a year ago had finally made a principled decision to watch the news anywhere else because her manner irritated him beyond measure. "I am an easygoing man," he once told Cindi. "I take things in stride. I try to exhibit the fruit of the Spirit. I don't fluster really. So why does this woman make me want to jump up and down on the hassock here, yelling and waving the remote?"

Cindi had been unsympathetic to his dilemma. "Because you watch the news on Channel 4? Instead of switching it?"

News Babe was suddenly back in front of him, and the sympathetic image of an unsympathetic Cindi faded. "Are you acquainted with the details of the scandal at Camel Creek?"

"No, ma'am," he said. "Not really."

"May we tell the public what your business might be here?"

"As soon as the public has a right to know."

Pastor Mitchell was at his shrewd best, and was thinking in a straight and narrow line. *Why are you asking* me *questions is my own little private thought here. For all you know, I am just here to pick up my joojoo-beans cancer treatment. For all you know, I am the electrician come to repair the short in the twenty-first century muscle relaxer and mind reader, the one with blinking lights. I am on to your sexy ways and tricks, you . . . you . . . woman with perfect teeth and gossip truck. Hah! For all* you *know, I am a Reformed Baptist pastor with credible inside connections to the monkeyshines at Camel Creek and, you know, I think I will be making my way inside.*

Which he did, and News Babe turned back to her engineer. "Those levels okay?" A few days later, Pastor Mitchell found out that he had been on the news that evening, with his cryptic comment on the public's apparent lack of a right to know being introduced by News Babe saying that "well-placed observers" are being tight-lipped about this whole situation. She ran with that clip because Mystic Union had declined to be interviewed on camera and would hold out for two additional days.

Mystic Union held out because while she, the former Mrs. Winmore, had a set of unique and murky perspectives on the care and treatment of virtually every ailment, not to mention almost total confusion with regard to the appropriate laws of inference, almost to the point of thinking that wet streets cause rain, this did not obscure her clear-sighted view of the main chance, and her clear knowledge that she currently had a shot at the main chance. She was dedicated to the proposition that Robert P. Warner had a winning lottery ticket in his clammy little hand, and she was resolved to hold the other hand encouragingly. And to occasionally pat it while giving sound, strategic advice.

The doors closed silently behind Pastor Mitchell, and he stood still for a moment, letting his eyes adjust to the darkness inside. The two policemen were standing in the foyer entrance, and both greeted him warmly. They shook his hand, congratulated him on his courageous and public-spirited performance outside, and introduced themselves. He did the same, and after a few minutes exchanging small talk, they all began to look around. They were in a combination foyer/bookstore/magazine stand, near the back of which was a doorway filled with hippie beads hanging down just like they did in the seventies.

Suddenly Charles Peaborne burst through the hippie beads and walked briskly past them, headed back for the front door.

He had not managed to see Robert P. Warner—who was still asleep, exhausted as he was from a late night of blogging about the loneliness of urban angst as recorded by French filmmakers, subtitling their angst like crazy, although the existential anguish was redeemed and ameliorated somewhat by plenty of full French frontal nudity, which he felt translated well without the subtitles, at least for him—but Peaborne *had* obtained a brief audience with Mystic Union. She had allowed it in order to provide him with some quotations that might be in their mutual interest and had obtained his e-mail address. Charles was elated and regarded his contact with these new allies as a profound vindication of his stand in the invoice-filing dispute of three years prior. When he had gotten some sleep, he could resume killing ants with his baseball bat. Out the door he went, trailing clouds of glory.

The pastor and two policemen made their way through the clickety beads and were greeted by two servant girls in white robes, wearing a couple of silver Halloween princess tiaras. The girls bowed down before them and then, rising, turned and escorted them toward the back wall. They both walked with the stately air that they imagined ancient servants might have used when escorting the Queen of Sheba to see Solomon, although the effect on an educated observer was not *quite* what they imagined. To their right and left were various alcoves, cubicles, and cubbies, in which crystals were waved, herbs were ingested, and hoobah dust was sprinkled, as the circumstances demanded and required. From one of the alcoves in the back

right, they could all hear a low groaning. But Mystic Union was
seated there against the back wall, holding court, and waiting to
receive her second wave of visitors. Bradford noticed in passing
that one of the servant girls had an Oakland Raiders tattoo on
her right ankle, which caused him to think that this joint might
not be all bad.

Mystic Union held up her right hand in greeting, and in such
a way as to forestall unnecessary preliminary chatter. "I am willing to see you briefly," she said. "But one of my many callings
is that of midwife, and I have a client I have to see almost immediately." And so it was that the low groaning was explained.

"You are a midwife *too*?" said Bradford.

"Why are you surprised? Modern medical conventions have
virtually turned childbirth into a disease. But it is nothing of
the kind. Did you know that there are places in the world where
women can just drop the child in the field, and go on with the
harvest? What does that suggest to you?"

"Third world? Grinding poverty? Gross infant mortality rates?"
Bradford guessed.

"*No.* It means that childbirth is natural, and not an event that
has to be conducted in a hospital. I am here to help women
understand how *natural* this is. But I will have to go in just a
moment. How may I help you?"

Rourke had delivered at least three babies in the back seats of
cars and taxi cabs, and thought he was qualified to assert that
there was nothing whatever that was natural about it. It was
the craziest thing in the world. Women were the kind of people

that *people* came out of, for crying out loud, and he thought it was the kind of thing best monitored by world-class doctors and sophisticated electronic gear, maintained closely by teams of nurses with graduate degrees in astrophysics. But that was just his opinion.

The detectives nodded first at Pastor Mitchell, who had finally figured out while parking his car the way he was going to ask his question. When he finally spoke, Mystic Union looked at him directly for the first time and started, and then flushed very slightly. He briefly nodded to her and introduced himself again. "Good morning," he said. "I don't know if you remember me . . . I am Pastor Mitchell at Grace Reformed."

But by the time he was done with his sentence, Mystic Union had recovered completely and said, "Yes, yes, of course. We all come to the mountain by various paths. But we all ascend the mountain. How may I help you?"

Pastor Mitchell caught himself being distracted by the fortune-cookie profundities, but concluded that he ought to refrain from saying anything about it. So he stayed on message. "Several months ago, my elders asked me to try to find out how best to dispense with the books left behind at the church by your ex-husband. They are boxed up in our church basement, and some of them are quite valuable. We do not really feel at liberty to dispose of them on our own authority. Do you know who would be in a position to make a decision?"

Mystic Union shook her head. "My husband's family members are all deceased and there is no one on my side who would want them. The books were very, um, *narrow.* They were even narrow by your Christian standards, and *that's* saying something. But the terms of the divorce settlement—given his, um, condition—left such things up to my discretion. You may dispose of them as seems best to you. Is that all?"

Pastor Mitchell nodded. "That is what I wanted to ask you. But if your new circumstance with Camel Creek leaves you in a position where you need to talk to someone from your old life, I would be happy to do so." He then gave her his card and looked at the detectives.

"Morning, ma'am," Rourke said. "What we would like to do is arrange an interview with Robert P. Warner. We understand that you . . . um, manage his schedule."

Mystic Union nodded, pleased. "Yes, that is what I do. Robert has been so terribly wounded by these events—by this betrayal of pastoral trust—that I have to be very careful about how much public exposure he gets. He is very frail."

"There is not a criminal case opened on this situation, and so please understand we are not at all insisting on anything. But we would appreciate it if you would allow us to visit with Robert. Here is my card." Rourke phrased it the way he did because he knew that the DA was as much interested in the main chance as Mystic Union was, and he, Rourke, was not really interested in that kind of political showboating. So he was therefore interested in touching all the bases he had to touch without actually pushing hard. If a case were opened, then all the normal rules would apply, and he would be more at ease.

Until then, he was going to do what he had to do without really going the extra mile.

Mystic Union took the card, nodded, and stood up. "I have to go," she said. "I will consider it."

THOSE DARN BACK RUBS

Lovers and madmen have such seething brains,
such shaping fantasies.
Theseus, *A Midsummer Night's Dream*

JOHNNY QUINN SAT IN HIS CUBICLE in the WildLife 4 Youth Rampage offices, but was not fully sure whether that was the right name. They kept changing the name on the brochures, so it was hard to know from day to day what the ministry was called. Uncertainty was part of the appeal. That was just one problem with ministering to the youth of today—riding the wave of cool and contemporary youth ministry was like surfing the big ones, and with one false move, there you were with sand in your trunks.

Johnny was rubbing the back of his neck. He was one of seven assistants to the main youth minister, who was off doing stuff and never around anymore, and Johnny had been told many times that he had a promising future ahead of him in this "most important work." He had short, blond hair and a diamond-stud earring—big enough to give him street cred, so necessary in youth work these days, and yet the earring was small enough to not worry the small handful of people at Camel Creek who *might* possibly have a problem with it. At one point in the church's history, there might have been a handful of people disturbed by this kind of thing in the church, but they had all died and gone to heaven quite a number of years before. Frankly, none of those people cared about it now, apparently having better things to think about. But Johnny still agonized over such things—what size earring would the apostle Paul have worn if his mission had been to the skateboarding and pants-droopy youth of today? Not an easy question to answer.

Every month or so the stress of youth ministry—dealing with the kids and *all* their issues—would get to Johnny, and so he would head on over to Brandy's apartment to have her give him a neck rub, followed by her specialty back rub. But somehow her giving him a back rub always turned into him giving her a front rub, and then they would *fall* again.

That was actually how their relationship started, which is to say, through those darn back rubs. It was her senior year in high school, and she was in Johnny's youth group, which was a combination Bible study and daisy-chain back-rub circle. At the end of that year, they all had a good working knowledge of the gospel of Mark and significantly improved blood flow in the delts. Brandy gave him a few back rubs back then that brought them perilously close to the edge, but honestly, there was no front rubbing until after she graduated and got her job at KING radio. That meant that when they finally followed the manner of all the earth, they were not violating the professional standards of youth ministry, but simply the seventh item on an ancient list which was from the Old Testament anyway.

They would always confess their fall afterward, and both of them remained entirely and blissfully unaware of what was causing it. They would both try hard to improve, which of course involved reading Scripture together, holding hands, and putting their heads closely together and praying about it. But somehow putting their heads together in this way didn't really help all that much, particularly when Brandy had on the perfume he really liked, and when his mouth got anywhere near her ear, which it usually did. The more they prayed about it like this, the worse things seemed to get. Anyhow, their periodic lapses had become almost a routine, and both of them had kind of adjusted to it.

Besides, there were lots of times in the month when they weren't doing it. But the whole scenario did make Johnny have to adjust his talk for the kids on abstinence, euphemisms, and indirect evasions now abounding everywhere, because he was not so hardened that he was capable of the hypocrisy on stilts that the senior ministry seemed to have mastered. Not that he knew anything about *that*, of course. Everything he urged upon the kids was still technically true, and the salient facts about his own testimony, as now phrased, were *technically* honest.

This is where Johnny's screensaver calendar came in. Each day had a new Bible verse floating around on the monitor, and the day after the scandal at Camel Creek did the mushroom cloud thing, the verse that arrested his attention, that actually *riveted* his attention, was the one about how the nation of Israel was defeated by the inhabitants of Ai—all because of Achan—and how Achan brought his "sin into the camp."

Johnny, despite his staggering ignorance of what was and what was not a turn-on to his girlfriend, was really a sincere fellow. As soon as he saw that verse, he knew that he was the Achan. Their senior pastor was an accused man, denying all charges vehemently and twisting in the wind because of him. Johnny was the kind of young man who could have read or written *Gullible's Travels* in one sitting, and he believed all those denials of Pastor Chad's with a whole heart. "But if such a charge were made against *me*," Johnny wondered, "what would I do? What could I say?"

The two of them had fallen just last week. Their sin *had* to be the cause of this scandal falling upon his beloved church. The rumors about the policemen visiting had swept through the administrative staff at Camel Creek, and their presence at the midweek service had not exactly gone unnoticed either. Everyone was rattled by the whole situation, and Johnny was a sincere staff member in the church with something on his conscience. *I am the Achan here. I am the one with dog doo on the shoe of personal holiness. Behold the man. Icky homo. Something like that.*

It takes special gifts to be a youth minister, and Johnny had them all. It takes remarkable gifts to be an *outstanding* youth minister, and Johnny had all those too. The second set of gifts adds up to an ability to hide the stark and off-putting nature of the first set of gifts. Youth ministers are young men who resent having graduated from high school when they were finally going to start hitting their stride in about three months, at least in the imaginations of their own hearts. They had never quite made the grade back then, particularly with the nubile young seventeen-year-old girls who were always so plentiful in those classes dedicated to teaching seventeen-year-olds generally. The problem was that the boys were also seventeen, and there is no clearer mismatch in the universe than a seventeen-year-old girl and a seventeen-year-old boy, another divine sense of humor thing. The clear thing to do when you are just out of college, then, is *return* to high school and resume the fight to gain the admiration of seventeen-year-old girls, but this time with a five-year advantage going. A twenty-two-year-old dope can sometimes appear—when the lighting is just right—as somewhat mature and not half bad, especially when the cute seventeen-year-old girls are being distracted and appalled by the current crop of seventeen-year-old boys.

And when the blind lead the blind, they both fall into a youth ministry. The theology of this gets somewhat complicated, but nothing else accounts for the steady stream of twenty-two-year-old cases of arrested development, baseball caps pointed in funny directions, into the burgeoning field of youth ministry. So that is one of the gifts that is requisite for young men in the field—the ability to seem like a peer who has his act together—and Johnny had this going for him.

The second gift was his ability to look as though this was not his motivation at all. To the kids in the group, and to their parents, on the rare occasions when parents actually met him, Johnny seemed to be devoted to youth ministry for the sake of the Great Commission. The only one who knew that he was sometimes a little diverted from bringing the gospel to the nations was Brandy, and she didn't mind, so long as they confessed it afterward.

Brandy was really sincere too, and when Johnny came to her, stricken in his conscience, she actually agreed with him that he really did need to talk to the policemen. He showed her the verse about Achan, was nearly stumbled by the perfume and her left ear again, but held up the shield of faith and quenched the fiery darts of the evil one.

He went over to the main office of the church, and Sharon Atwater gave him the names of the cops, along with their phone numbers. She was frantically curious about why he wanted them, but was keeping her head low and was still not-for-Chadding. So she said nothing, nothing at all. Zilch. As soon as the second hand swept by the appropriate number on the clock, she was out of there.

So late in the afternoon it was, and Johnny sat down by his phone in his office, closed the door three times, checked the latch twice, and tried to spit out the cotton balls that had mysteriously filled up his mouth. He fooled around for fifteen minutes this way, and finally got his toes over the edge of the high dive platform, took six deep breaths, four rapid and shallow ones, closed his eyes, and put the receiver to his ear. Beep beep boop . . . boop boop . . . *ahhh* . . . beep . . . *akk* . . . beep.

"MPD, Bradford," came an authoritative voice. It was the voice of God's minister of wrath, the avenging angel, coming to strike down all the firstborn. Johnny was firstborn, which was part of his problem, but pursuit of those issues would take us too far afield.

"Yes, hello," said Johnny, his voice covering several octaves almost simultaneously. "I am on staff here at Camel Creek, and wondered if it would be possible to arrange an interview with you?"

The voice on the other end became even more professional, were that possible, and arranged a time for the following day when Johnny could meet with Bradford and Rourke. Johnny didn't want to do it on the church grounds since Achan was brought to justice outside the camp, and volunteered to come down to the police department. Bradford said that this would be fine.

It has to be admitted that Bradford was expecting far more from the interview than what they actually wound up getting. He thought that a staff member in the know had finally cracked, and was going to come down to the station and sing, as they used to say in the old movies, like a bird. What they actually got was a frightened young man who believed that he was the only one in the history of Camel Creek, or perhaps in the city, to have ever sinned in this fashion.

Rourke was an old-school Catholic, so he didn't really follow the Achan references. If it wasn't in Latin, he thought, there was a certain impiety in paying attention. But Bradford had been reared in a different kind of old-school thought, and as a youth had been regularly whacked about the head and shoulders with the story of Achan, and Saul and the Amalekites, and how Agag got hewn to pieces in the presence of the Lord, and how Uzzah should have kept his hands in his pockets. The point of these stories had been pressed home to him by the kind of preachers who rolled up their shirtsleeves, threw their necktie over the right shoulder, and hopped around while they preached. Many Americans have complained of too many hellfire and damnation sermons in their past, but Bradford was one of the 112 individuals in our generation who had actually heard one. He was thirteen at the time and was a pretty good boy for five days afterward. So Bradford was thoroughly conversant on the Achan thing.

At the same time, he was a little disappointed. The guts having been spilled, and Achan having been explained to Rourke (twice), the end result was that Johnny honestly confessed to being the only one who had ever sinned in this way at Camel Creek. All others were saintly—some of them, including Pastor Chad, having two halos—and were far more focused than he was on the ever-present task of evangelization. As far as gushing with salacious details about the activities of the senior pastor went, Johnny was a dry hole.

The two policemen just slumped and listened to the tale of woe. A diligent Catholic and a lapsed fundamentalist sat slack-jawed and stared as Johnny outlined his view of why these charges had been brought against Chad Lester. "Brandy agrees with me," he finally said, by way of confirmation. The two detectives were flummoxed, but both of them, unbeknownst to the other, had noticed an odd expression in one of Johnny's statements and saw something they needed to follow up on later. Johnny had said, in a throwaway kind of way, that "Pastor Lester had once said in a Bible study with all the youth ministers that this sort of thing was 'normal,' whatever that meant."

When the torturous saga was over, Rourke just looked at Bradford helplessly. *I know I am the senior cop here, but you have to run with this one. You are no Mother Teresa, or the Protestant equivalent, as the whole department well knows, but you apparently have some idea of what the hell this young sap is saying.* Rourke had expressive eyes. Bradford scratched his chin thoughtfully. Two things.

"Two things," he said. "First, when it comes to the issues of spiritual warfare, our department is not really authorized to make any final determinations. I am sure you understand. But I will make note of your confession, and it *will* be in our file on this case." Bradford made a mental note that his doodle in the upper right hand corner of the interview sheet with Sharon Atwater would constitute that note. "We are not saying anything one way or the other about your view that this behavior of yours is the cause of the accusation against your pastor. If it is, then presumably this confession should turn things around for you, or at least allay your conscience." Johnny nodded eagerly. An allayed conscience. That was the ticket.

But then, on his second point, Bradford launched into some new territory for the MPD and said a few things that caused Rourke to swear at him for a little bit in the hallway afterward. Bradford could tell that this young man thought of them both as Authorities, in the high, rarified, Romans 13 sense. He could also tell that Johnny was not really a highly trained logician, and would simply go as he was directed, as long as the suggested direction did not conflict with the tangled bundle of platitudes, loosely tied with string, that made up his worldview.

"What you need to do," Bradford said, "is ask this young Brandy to marry you. Then you can fool around as much as you want, and no more senior pastors will ever topple from their perch because of you. You like her, right?"

Johnny's eyes were round, like a couple of trash can lids, only a different color. As much as he liked Brandy as a friend, and a friend who was a girl, and okay, a girlfriend, and periodic co-sinner, the idea of marriage had never entered his head. He was not a long-range thinker, and next week's activities and associated Bible lesson were about as far as it went. Marriage involved *years,* or so he had heard. And yet, here was this officer of the law, a man who now was in possession of all the facts, telling him to go in this direction.

He swallowed nervously. "Are you telling me I have to do this?"

Rourke looked at Bradford menacingly.

"No, I am *not* telling you to do this," Bradford said. "But given what you have told us, what is the *right* thing to do?" Bradford had never felt this pastoral before, and he kind of liked it. Brandy owed him big time.

This did not make Rourke any happier, as the subsequent hallway discussion indicated, but it seemed to settle the matter for Johnny. "I will think and pray about it. I will have to look at what I am earning. There are so many things to think about . . ." He trailed off.

"Yes, but one of them will no longer be the question of whether *happy* times for Johnny mean *sad* times for one of your spiritual superiors the following morning."

The logic of this, given Johnny's premises, was unassailable, and deep within his heart, the tumbler clicked. He would do it. *Okay.* Got to check some things first, but he would still do it. He unrolled his baseball cap, stood up, stuck it on his head, and put out his hand. "Thank you," he said. "Thank you."

"Glad to be of service," Bradford said. He meant it too.

Rourke was civil to Johnny and opened the door for him. After it closed behind him, Rourke counted to fifteen to get Johnny a little farther down the hallway. At sixteen, his intent was to give his junior partner unshirted hell for leaving the path of detective work and becoming a lonely hearts guy.

He was clearing his throat and deciding whether to stand on the chair or not, when Bradford held up his hand, looking for all the world like a minister about to deliver a benediction. "I know," he said. "But there is no need to thank me. It is just a gift. My mother thought I was destined for the ministry actually."

Rourke spun around and stomped out the door. Bradford followed him out. "Don't you agree? We really need to do our part to reduce this epidemic of illicit banging in the evangelical world. Before this week, I had no idea. Back in Arkansas, we were all good Christians until we got our drivers' licenses. After that we were good pagans. It is this mixing of categories that I find so troublesome."

DEEP COMMUNICATING

I went to the river to jump in,
My baby showed up and said, "I will tell you when."
Tore Down

MICHELLE LESTER HAD DECIDED about a half an hour after the scandal broke that she and her daughters, Kimberly and Shannon, were going to go up to their mountain condo for the weekend in order to do some journaling, grieving, and deep communicating. There were so many *issues,* and there always seemed to be *more,* no matter what they did, or how fast or how much they wrote in their journals. The girls were used to this process and really would have been fine about the whole thing, except that each one of the girls thought the other one was going to bring the pot. Turned out neither of them brought it, and there they were, confronted with a long weekend of quality time with their mother, without any assistance from the world of herbal remedies.

Michelle had called Brian about the weekend away, and he had encouraged her to go. He said he would miss her and asked what time they should connect again on Monday. He was so nice—the only thing that was worrisome about him was his attraction to that Mitchell church. They had only talked about that a few times, and Brian was apparently far less noncommittal about it in his conversations with *her* than he was in his conversations with Pastor Mitchell. He was far more interested in that church than Mitchell could have guessed, and Michelle knew it. She had never attended Grace Reformed with him, and was quite content with the perceptions she had formed at fifty yards. She wasn't really going to church anywhere, but she remained a contemporary evangelical to the back teeth. She had lost her faith while still managing to hang on to all the platitudes.

As the weekend approached, Michelle had developed a more specific goal for their time together. It had begun with an abstract faith in the act of journaling, but there was a real decision looming up ahead of her that she needed to think through. There was an important aspect of the divorce settlement where she had not yet decided what to do, and she hoped that rehearsing and rehashing the whole debacle with the girls would push her over the edge.

So the three of them—Michelle, Shannon (the elder), and Kimberly (the younger)—dropped their bags just inside the front door of the condo and headed out for a bite to eat. They were within walking distance of a number of upscale eateries and had no trouble picking out a little bistro with espresso and ferns, the kind of place that served exotic little art sandwiches with bark still in the bread. The only problem with these places was that there were always waiters there named Chad, and that kind of kept the tender issues right on the surface.

After they were seated, Michelle folded her hands together and said, "Girls, we need to talk through these issues concerning your father because we really need each other. I know we have the inner resources to get through this." Her facial expressions and cadences were just like Oprah, only a great deal whiter.

The girls just looked at her blankly, although Michelle had no idea that this is what they were doing. They knew better than to argue with this kind of girl time together, so they just did what they always did, which was to blink occasionally, followed by a nod. Their father had taken all their oxygen years before when he went philandering over the horizon, and when natural forces, abhorring a vacuum, restored some of the oxygen, their mother took it away by other helpful and certified means, clustering round with a suffocating blanket of therapeutic clichés. Still, she was a devoted mother, which meant that the girls were simultaneously appreciative and at their wits' end. They were good students, because they both thought this meant that it would increase their chances of going to college a long way away, and then hooking up with a man who had come to college from a long way in the opposite direction.

Michelle was a smart woman, but it must also be said she had always been a "will that be on the test?" kind of smart. She had a perfect score on the verbal portion of her SAT test, and was no slouch on the math portion either. She had gone to college on a full-ride academic scholarship, and had been pretty ambitious, if that modest phrase is elastic enough to cover being *very* ambitious. All of this, along with some corollaries, was about to tumble out of her because Michelle had come to the condo that weekend prepared to share *way* too much with her daughters. They had gone through some journaling marathons a couple times before, but Michelle had always held back, thinking it the principled thing to do. But now she had resolved to be completely transparent. Michelle's grandmother, a grand dame of the old school in Mississippi, would have said that Michelle was about to go stepping in high cotton.

In college, Michelle had occasionally daydreamed about one day being the First Lady, but was humble enough (to herself) to not be *too* set on it. She was naturally beautiful, but over the years she had minor cosmetic surgery on several occasions, including a couple of Barbie implants. She belonged to the fitness club, had a personal trainer, and was always slightly, winsomely, tanned. She was blonde naturally, but was not above giving herself a nudge in that direction from time to time.

"About two years after I found out about your father's behavior, as you know, I met Brian. *Such* a considerate man. What you don't know is that his consideration has been a sharp contrast in *every* area."

The field of high cotton was approaching, but so was the waiter, a young man named Chad; no relation. He stopped next to the table and remained quiet, as many waiters do, to give the conversationalists a moment to wind down. But Michelle had launched into the first part of the monologue she had prepared and appeared oblivious to his presence. *He,* however, was very aware of his presence there, as were the two daughters.

"After your grandfather passed away, your father was impotent for about six months. So selfish, *so* self-absorbed. I spoke to him about it a number of times, sometimes quite forcefully . . ."

Chad cleared his throat. "Excuse me? May I share with you what we have on special?"

The two girls looked at him with grateful and pleading eyes. *Tell us* all *the specials the restaurant has* ever *had.* In the conversational break that followed, while the waiter was talking, Michelle blinked a couple times and thought over the scenario again. After Michelle had found out about Chad's infidelities, she had drifted into her adultery with Brian, who had been her investment broker. Unlike her husband, who was apparently doing everything he could to cover the waterfront, she was faithful to her new lover, and he was faithful to her. Brian was still an unbeliever, but a decent sort. She had initially felt bad about sleeping with someone who didn't have a testimony, but she got over it soon enough.

". . . and the blackened catfish, with our special Cajun sauce."

They all looked at Chad the waiter blankly, but it looked to him like they were looking at him thoughtfully, and Michelle's thoughts were wandering again. Michelle had initially taken up with Brian as an act of attempted "take *that*" revenge on Chad, but then lost her nerve when she was going to tell Chad about it. She had initially assumed the information would devastate Chad, but on the threshold of telling him, suddenly realized that it probably would not do anything of the kind. Then, after *that*, she found that she was emotionally attached to Brian, and the Lester marriage staggered ineptly toward the point of divorce.

Chad the waiter left them with their menus, along with the information about the specials, and retreated quietly. Shannon and Kimberly watched him go with sadness, and Michelle started up again.

"Some forms of selfishness are bearable, and in the give-and-take of *any* relationship, you certainly have to deal with it. But selfishness in lovemaking is simply unendurable. And that is what I *told* him, a number of times."

The two helpless daughters began thinking that perhaps that boy back in school really knew what he was talking about when he would alert the class with his constant refrain of "Overshare!" Shannon, in an attempt to get the subject off things she didn't want to know about, had to resort to asking about things she did know about.

"Tell us again about how the news about Dad went over at the church. I . . . I was too much in shock to notice very much then."

Of course, in the church, the announcement of the impending divorce was amicably and professionally accomplished, as it pretty much had to be, and the repercussions did not seriously affect Chad's ministry at all. In fact, he got a book deal with Zondervan out of it—*Walking With Christ Through Divorce.* If John Mitchell had been at the next table talking to Cherie, in one of his periodic and vain attempts to get through to her, he would have told her that the congregation at Camel Creek had gotten such a steady diet of relational goo from Chad's messages that they were fully prepared to accept the "growing apart" line, along with the "still best of friends" bit. And Cherie would have said to him, "You're always so negative, John. Cranky, almost." But he wasn't there, so none of that happened.

Michelle was focusing intently on her daughters, wanting them to hear everything she said, regardless of what she said. They had come up here to this place to *share*. "The elders had me meet with that counselor of theirs a few times, just so they could say they had checked that box, and I knew that, but I told the counselor about everything anyway."

"Even about, about the . . ." Kimberly started to ask.

"The impotence? Of course. *Especially* about the impotence. I told the elders about that too, just to see some of them smirk and turn red. Two of them in particular, who might have been tempted to think that he was such a studly dudley."

Shannon thought her mother was shouting the word *impotence* and looked up at her second use of it to see that Chad the waiter was right there, right on time, to take their order. He stood there, looking as solemn as a judge, for which the girls were thoroughly grateful. He attended a small charismatic church in the area, and for him, dealing with *overshare* was a way of life, an art form.

But after Chad the waiter receded with their orders, the girls turned back to their mother, interested in spite of themselves. "Two of the *elders*?"

Like her husband, Michelle had been a perfectionist, and when it became apparent that her marriage was not a suitable venue for a perfectionist to practice her arts, she had turned her attention to their two girls. Michelle had become the uber-mom and was involved up to her chin in developmental activities for her daughters—ballet, soccer, violin, therapy, soccer, and more therapy. The girls had always done well at King's Academy Christian School, which was sponsored by Camel Creek in more ways than one. It *was* an academically sound school, but it had long ago lost all moral authority with the students. The one rule that was enforced was that any moral disorder must not be conducted in such a way as to embarrass the headmaster in the newspapers, and for the most part the students honored this working truce with the administration.

Both daughters were quasi-regular users of marijuana (but anything harder would be stupid), and both had slept with several of their classmates. They had been careful not to get pregnant (which would have embarrassed the school and church in the newspapers), but felt completely free to do whatever they wanted to do. They did not want to wreck their lives, but they did want to suit themselves. They were accomplished musicians, decent athletes, and decent students. Their mother was thoroughly invested in their development, which they both knew, and so they did not really detest their mother. It would be more accurate to say they tolerated their mother with affection, sandpapering the rough spots of their relationship with a little help from some hippie's illegal garden. The worst part was having to do all that damn journaling, and here they were with a whole weekend stretching out in front of them like a very straight highway in Wyoming, the only bend in the road involving the very slight curvature of the earth. But the waiter who had seated them (not Chad the waiter, but the first employee to greet them behind the lectern thing; the one who said "Table for three?" and carried the silverware) looked like he might have some connections with Colombian agriculture. If not, the next rest area was fifty-eight miles.

The girls had detested their father since they found out about his adulteries, but what their mother was telling them now awakened the first glimmer of sympathy that either one had ever had for him. Of course, it would be easy for good Christians everywhere to detest Chad, joining right in with the Lester women on this point, because, taking one thing with another, he was, well, detestable. But even creeps have hopes, dreams, aspirations. Even creeps have a story and perhaps a brief moment in their toddler years when they were cute. Michelle thought she was giving the girls the back story, the information that would make their detestation and bitterness mature. It was actually having the opposite effect. But of course, Rome wasn't built in a day.

"I am certainly not making excuses for him, but your father grew up with an indulgent mother and a severe, distant, and demanding father. You girls don't remember them. Everyone who knows your father knows that he was born a CEO, and his gifts were manifested early on in student government in high school and college. Half the faculty thought he was an inevitable and tragic choice in running for governor. He had *everything* in control except for his relationship with his father, who was impossible to please."

This was quite true, if something else might be inserted here. The more Chad exhibited control of his grades, ambitions, hair, junior high Day-timer, briefcase, and other sundry accomplishments, the more his father withheld approval. This battle between them was actually a battle for fundamental control of their relationship, and a year after Chad graduated from college, his father triumphed in their running battle by dying of a massive heart attack, leaving Chad with no real way to get back on the scoreboard.

"So after we graduated, we got married. I figured out *later* that this was so that Chad could say 'take *that*' to his father. Your grandmother was formidable but, um, plain. I was homecoming queen—did you know that?—oh, of course."

Things were quiet at the table for a few moments. The girls played with their napkins.

"He was a virgin when we married," Michelle said suddenly. Shannon and Kimberly looked around in alarm for Chad the waiter, but he was inexplicably at another table. "I wasn't, but only because of the youth pastor at my home church. And what a lecherous goat *he* was. He made it to the big time, though. He is some kind of wheel at Families International now."

If Chad the waiter had been there for the whole conversation, and if he had been a trained counselor, he might have been able to read between the lines and say that, despite everything, things were not exactly a train wreck in the Lester marriage, depending on what kind of scale you use, until Chad's father died. That death had thrown Chad into a deep blue aquamarine funk, and his resultant bout of impotence. Michelle had said she had spoken to him firmly about it, but it would be closer to the point to say she taunted him mercilessly over it, which led eventually to Chad's sexual rebellion and the manifestation of this new (and inevitable) area of his life which he could not control. A control freak everywhere else, his father had thoroughly taught him that if there had to be *one* area where he had to be helpless, it might as well be an area with some short-term rewards.

"When I met your father at Camel Creek, that was back when it was Evangelical Alliance Church. We both grew up in severely conservative homes, and so we both liked the contemporary worship. Your father had told me that he was going to be the governor someday, which *I* took as a promise, and we were preparing for law school, but then the church asked him to reorganize the youth ministry. And a year after his father died, the pastor of the church retired, and your father was asked to consider the post. He had never been to seminary, but the church only had several hundred people in it, and they really liked his easy, conversational style of speaking. And he was a hard-driving organizer behind the scenes. And credit where it's due, he was *good*."

"And then what?" Kimberly asked.

"He had promised me to run for governor. I finally said okay to the church offer, assuming our agreement there was for just a short-term thing. But within six months, the attendance at the church had exploded."

An hour later, Michelle folded her hands primly on her lap. "There. I am glad we came. Let's go back to the condo. We can all do some journaling for a little bit and then share before we go to bed." The girls nodded gamely, and they all got up to go. When they all got out to the parking lot, Kimberly pretended to have left her purse inside, and said, "Hold on a sec," and dashed back in to ask the waiter at the lectern her question. She had clearly misjudged her man, because she came back out after a moment with her purse and shook her head slightly at Shannon. No dope to be had. The three walked slowly down the sidewalk back to their place, all three chatting aimlessly.

Michelle had unloaded so much information that she ought to have felt three or four pounds lighter. But she didn't, and she was no closer to her decision.

At the very moment when the Lester women were washing their sandwiches down with five-dollar bottles of water, Chad Lester was looking over his shoulder in a metaphorical sense. Not physically. Nothing was coming up from behind him *that* way. But he knew it was over. It had to be over. Nothing but over.

He had fallen off a skyscraper, and nothing really was to be done about it. What he did between now and the time he hit the sidewalk would not really affect things one way or the other. He needed to do what was necessary to do, and not just go through the motions. Perhaps it was not inevitable. But it probably was. Not so inevitable that he should not continue to work with the attorneys, the staff, and the authorities. But it was inevitable enough to not matter if he called Cherie, in search of a little warmth and sympathy that might become horizontal. Angela had been a disappointment and had really acted very selfishly. Cherie was a *warm* person. Of course, she had reacted very strongly when they drifted apart some years ago, but perhaps she would be willing to talk with him this afternoon. He had checked with Miguel, and as one of the pensioners, she had assured him of her continued silence. She had also appeared to understand that this meant that the pay scales would be adjusted. Miguel had said something about a balloon payment, but whatever. Perhaps she still had feelings, or needs, or something. Sure, why not call Cherie?

Around the time Michelle had been describing to their daughters, Chad's sexual flailing had been limited to motel porn and occasional strip clubs in other cities while away on business. But within several years of taking the pastorate at the church, now renamed Camel Creek, several observant women counselees had seen their opportunity and seduced him without very much difficulty at all. "Like hitting the floor with my hat," one of them said afterward to a friend. "Not that difficult." After those two fiascos, Chad tried to get ahead of his lack of control in this area by becoming the predator, creating an illusion of mastery to himself. His infidelities became known to Michelle after about ten years, and then had become an open secret to about half of the church staff and personnel. The other half continued with their labors in trying to fulfill the Great Commission.

Chad was a very capable speaker (he didn't really preach), and for those who liked that kind of schmoozing, he was *very* good at it. He was as good at speaking as a man who has fallen off a skyscraper can be. Those who did not care for this genre of speaking—like Pastor Mitchell, say, to take one sample at random—found it intolerable. Chad subscribed to CEO magazines, read business guru books, devoured the *Wall Street Journal*, and, while away on business trips, looked every inch the Fortune 500 businessman. Because of his salary, book deals, and so on, he had become a very wealthy and very put-together man. He had a very winsome smile, every hair was in place—without looking *too* much like helmet hair. He was immaculately tailored, but in a way that was always deliberately casual. He was never flustered or angry. In office matters, he always knew what to do and was the undisputed master of the elder board, ministry teams, and church staff. In one area of his life only, deeply hidden, was this sense of sexual panic. Why not call Cherie?

The weekend was approaching, and, speaking of control, Chad needed to go over his message for Sunday. He walked briskly down the corridors of Camel Creek's administrative wing and turned abruptly into the sermon-writers' office. There were nine writers in there—fewer than some of the other megachurches—and they were responsible to have Sunday's message delivered to his desk by noon on Friday. He usually did not look at it until he was actually delivering it, but after the "best positions for women" flameout the other night, he was rattled enough to go over it beforehand. The message was late, probably because they were trying to nuance the heck out of it. Of course, Chad had a certain measure of sympathy with their dilemma. How do you write a sermon for somebody in such—um, unique circumstances? And at least two of the writers were privy to information that *could* keep them from writing with great verve and moral authority under such circumstances. But those two whassnames had been okay in bed. Chad decided not to be angry about the message being late.

A few moments later, he was walking out to his car, fifteenth draft of the message in hand, and he found himself dialing Cherie as he pulled out of the parking lot. He began to leave a message on her answering machine, when she suddenly picked up.

"Hello?"

"Hello, Cherie. Chad here. I was wondering if you had a moment to talk. Can I swing by?"

PROPPING UP ROBERT P.

Conceit: God's gift to little men.
Bruce Barton

AFTER THE POLICE OFFICERS LEFT the Health Temple, Mystic Union spent a long afternoon with the woman in the back room who was in labor, a woman who finally produced a man child sunny side up, despite all attempts to keep it from happening the way it usually happens in nations with indoor plumbing. At the Health Temple, the best efforts were made to re-create conditions for mother and child that approximated the conditions found at higher altitudes in Nepal, and the effect of this was that both mother and child almost died several times, but since no one actually did, they happily departed the Temple late the next day, with no one the wiser.

When the delivery itself was accomplished, and the aftermath of the delivery settled down to a semblance of quiet, Mystic Union trudged slowly up the wooden stairs at the back of the

Temple. The steps were tucked away behind the painted scenery that made the usher girls feel like they were a couple of the chief feminine ornaments of Solomon's court, although Solomon would most likely have been nonplussed by the Raiders tat. Mystic Union had the self-assured glow of a job well done; her work accomplished, it was time for some herbal tea, and then a late dinner. She was pleased also by the fact that Mitchell had come that morning. The policemen had been expected, but he was most certainly not expected. What was his game? Another surprise was that Peaborne fellow, with the interesting offer of a working alliance. More than enough to think about. Good things happening here, and the horoscope concurred. The only stress in her life was waiting for her upstairs, good old Robert P. Warner. Mystic Union's soul did not have teeth, but if it had, they would have been gritted, and occasionally grinding. *If he doesn't have that thing written, I'll just do it.*

There was a landing near the top of the stairs which Mystic Union rounded, and then took the remaining three steps in a couple of bounds. Slouched across the decrepit sofa was her tattered lottery ticket out of there—Robert P. Warner II—poet, prophet, pasty blogger of the early a.m. The sofa was of the old gray mare swayback school of design, and from somewhere within the cushions, *de profundis,* came a groan from Robert P. He was disconsolate and had been listening for her steps on the landing for the last half hour or thereabouts. He timed his groan according to the short melodrama he had worked out as he lay there.

Pretending that her soul did not have dental issues, Mystic was all solicitude. "Love! What is the matter?"

Robert opened one rheumy eye, again according to drill, and greeted her as one greets the sole remaining person in one's life who is prepared to act sympathetically, which in fact, Mystic Union probably was.

He stifled another groan and got unsteadily to his feet. "Oh, not much to speak of. I spent a lot of time on that statement you wanted for the attorney . . ." He trailed off.

Mystic Union glanced over at the notepad that was on the kitchen table right behind the sofa and saw, even from that distance, that there was but a sentence or two on it. Not only did she see this, but Robert *saw* that she saw, and moved adroitly to the next barricade. "My carpal tunnel started acting up again . . . and I spent a lot of time hunting for my old brace." With this, he held up his right arm. "I found it in the box with my old journals from high school . . ." And he stopped.

Robert P. Warner II had been the kind of boy in high school who managed his injuries as a mother hen hovers over her chicks. He was a master of communicating physical distress to others, but the nature of the injury and the nature of the distress he would subsequently manifest were not really in accord with the laws of logic first outlined in such a cogent way by Aristotle. One time, when he had been beaned in the forehead by a volleyball in Mr. Walker's phys ed class, the injury, such as it was, resulted in a mild ringing in the ears. But this had translated, by the end of the period, into a clear limp; by the end of the day, into a striking limp; and by the next Monday morning, into a pair of crutches and a leg brace on the outside of his jeans. This was a violation of Aristotle's law of identity, an injury to the head being an injury to the head, and not, say, an injury to the right knee. The brace on his right hand at this very moment had been acquired under similar circumstances and in a similar way. He was glad he had found it under all those journals, which he had then spent a couple hours going through. Good stuff. It was amazing how insightful he had been in high school.

Mystic Union appeared to be all sympathy, but also managed, somehow, to be all business. "Dear, how you must have suffered . . . I am so sorry about your wrist, but you know, Robbie, that we really, really *must* have that statement for the attorney by Wednesday."

Robert actually knew this, and he nodded his head as though he knew this. The spirit was willing. It was not that he was incapable of writing—he had churned out millions of words for his blog. The physical activity of writing was nothing to him. When it came to pensive reflections of man and his existential condition (as mirrored in the experiences of Robert P.), foreign film reviews that were allowed to make as little sense as the films themselves, extended discussions of how the pert French breasts in those films could not really be deconstructed, Derrida or no Derrida, and long, protracted discussions of how people—particularly food service personnel—misunderstood him, Robert was a machine. If it was narcissism and self-indulgence you were after, he could write like a bat out of the bad place. The problem with this stupid statement for the attorney was that it had to conform to certain . . . objective realities. Robert was astute enough to know that a statement for his attorney was not to be a creative writing exercise, and so he had to stick to the facts. But he hardly knew any facts and was thus having trouble sticking to them.

The initial statement for their attorney, the one that had kicked off the suit, had been easy enough. It was only a paragraph long and about summed the whole thing up. Ten years prior, Robert had gone over to the Camel Creek offices in order to "see the pastor." He never attended church there and did not know one office from another, one pastor from another, or, for that matter, one thing from another. He was experimenting with Buddhism at the time and yet was feeling depressed. He was confused about his sexual identity and wanted someone to talk to, which is to say, he wanted to find someone who would listen to him talk. He had found himself sitting across the desk from the pastor, who found out about the sexual identity thing almost *right* away, and who took it from there. All of that was clear as day. Their tryst was burned in his memory much as a Circle R brand would have sizzled on the rump of a writhing calf. Out west. A hundred years or so ago. So to speak. He knew about all that from the movies.

When he told Mystic Union about it six months ago, she had come alive. Her eyes had sparkled, just like her crystal earrings that kept her in touch with her two grandmothers, now deceased. "Oh, *Robert,*" she had said. "We really need to do something about this. We should see an attorney . . . making these charges public is not tawdry at all. I see it as part of the healing process . . . that, and cornflake poultices."

So, inspired by the moment, Robert had written out the paragraph like nobody's business, and both Mystic Union and the attorney had assumed (wrongly) that when called upon, he would just open the spigot again, and all the other details would flow out. But when it came time to produce, Robert didn't. He didn't remember anything else, was unwilling to make things up in this legal context (having seen more than one daytime TV courtroom drama where bad things happened to people who did make them up), and he had quickly discovered that to research the subject—checking dates, getting corroboration for other details—looked and smelled suspiciously like work. Which is why he got carpal tunnel syndrome today. Yesterday he had twisted his ankle.

Suddenly a happy thought struck him. "When I was finding my brace, I said that I found some journals . . . I thumbed through them for just a minute and noticed how cheerful I was back then. This was before that pastor at Camel Creek took my childhood away from me. I bet I could get a few quotes from those journals that would make *that* point in quite an amazing way." But of course, in this, Robert was quite mistaken. He had not been cheerful back then, but, being young, had been comparatively ignorant of all the different and creative ways of being miserable. Now that Robert P. had been exploring those different ways for some years on his blog, the lack of scope exhibited in his high school years struck him as being full of sunshine. So he would write down some of the quotes tomorrow, and on Wednesday his attorney would just stare at him.

"That would be just wonderful, Robbie. I think that is a wonderful idea." Mystic Union just wanted to get him writing, perhaps now, and maybe the journal entries would prime the pump. But Robert wanted to blog instead, he wanted more than a little open field running for his emotions. No fences. No boundaries. No one to say *no*. If he wrote things down on that *notepad*, first thing you know bailiffs would be having him raising his right hand, and so-help-me-Goding, and the-whole-truthing, and nothing-but-the-truthing. And beyond what he had given already, he could find out no more apart from having to work on it. And besides, his wrist hurt.

Mystic Union was in the kitchen bending over the stove, fixing water for her tea, and rummaging through her canister of selections. "You want some tea, Robbie?" She was also rummaging through some ideas for how she could write Robert P.'s statement for him. Although Robert's grasp of the correspondence theory of truth was tenuous, it did exist. Mystic, it must be confessed, was not constrained in that regard in any way. And the attorney needed it.

An affirmative grunt came back regarding the tea, and Robert P. schlepped into the kitchen.

"What did you do today?" he asked. "Besides the baby, I mean?"

Mystic Union brightened and thought this might be an opportunity to stir the embers of Robert's lethargy with the iron poker of interesting coincidences. Not that she put it to herself that way, of course. The only thing she would have done with a metaphor like that would have been to bean Robert over the head with the poker.

"The policemen came," she said, "as I thought they would. I have a customer who works in the DA's office, and she told me in *strictest* confidence that old Radavic was furious about our suit the day after we filed it. So I thought I would see some policemen sometime."

Robert P. was staring down into his mug of green tea, wondering if he could blog anything about the little reflected shapes he could see floating on the surface. Mystic took this as a sign of meditative encouragement and said, "But the really interesting thing was the two other visitors. One was Charles Peaborne, who used to work at Camel Creek. He appears to be a man who is truly . . . truly *centered*. He wants to work together with us on this. He told me that Camel Creek is rotten to the core, which I suppose we already knew. But he spoke quite authoritatively."

Mystic Union, despite the informative crystals hanging from her ears, was not really in a position to critique the value of Mr. Peaborne's intelligence. But judging from the intensity of his obvious conviction and the shaky timbre of his voice when he spoke of "nefarious doings" and "speaking truth to power," she could only assume that he was in possession of the real goods. It would turn out later that his website would be devoted more to concerns about paper clip and toner cartridge misfeasance, malfeasance, and nonfeasance than anything else, but it would be best not to blame Mystic for not knowing this. After all, it was not like she was psychic or anything.

Robert looked up from his tea, his first blog post having been formed in his mind, and he pretended to show interest in what Mystic had been talking about. "Well, Mys," he said, "you said there was one other?"

"Ah, yes," she said. "Pastor Mitchell. He replaced my ex-husband as the pastor of Grace Reformed back in . . . back in . . . my previous life. I listened to him preach for a few months. He was a nice man, but I had decided long before he got there that I had had quite enough of *that,* thank you."

"So why did he come?"

"Well, he said it was about my ex-husband's books that were still at the church. But then he as much as told me that this was just an excuse for seeing me. He said that if I wanted to visit, he would be happy to. But I have no idea why he might want to do that. He knows I am connected to Lester's little difficulties, but what could *his* connection to them be?"

"So why don't you meet with him and find out?"

Dinner, as Mystic had anticipated, was a little late. It was a slab of white tofu on a crimson plate, with a few cashews sprinkled on the top. Robert looked at his meal, heartsick, aware that this was the price he had to pay for all the other perks attainable nowhere else, like a roof over his head and sex from time to time. But he didn't mind the tofu so much as he minded having to interrupt his blogging after Mystic was in bed in order to walk down to the corner 7-Eleven for his 32-ounce bag of Doritos.

And he had to eat them all on the way back too, because Mystic had strong opinions on what she found in her trash cans.

The evening dragged out. Conversation lagged, even before it began drooping. Then the evening dragged some more. Then, unbelievably, there was even more boring stretches later. After nine, they both went to bed for some listless and perfunctory sex, after which Robert P. got up again to watch a couple videos he had rented earlier. They were both deep videos, and Robert was so confused by them that when he fired up the computer for some blogging, he was really ready to roll. First, he knocked out the piece on green tea that he had thought through earlier. Then he went on to write about the angst he felt whenever he quoted Sartre, although he was unsure whether the angst caused the quoting, or the quoting caused the angst. Whatever. Ham and eggs. After that was his Dorito break, washed down with a liter of Mountain Dew, with all the evidence tossed in the dumpster behind the Health Temple (that was shared with a neighboring apartment house, so he was okay).

When he came back, he was ready to review the movies, but first thought that he needed to check his blogging stats. In the week before the civil suit, his monthly average was about thirty visits a month. And, to be fair, about half of those were from his sister in Memphis who was *so* proud. The day the Camel Creek story broke, there had been three hundred visits in one day. And the next day, after the wire services picked it up, there had been three thousand visits and twenty-five thousand hits as visitors flailed around trying to find something about Camel

Creek. But of course, there was nothing there about the scandal. Mystic had been insistent on that point—she was not too bright, but she was shrewd—and so Robert was now back to writing for his usual audience, whoever they were.

The first movie was *The Cry of Doucette*. The second was like unto the first, only more so. The title, roughly translated, meant something like *The Green Lentils of Despair*. He began typing furiously:

4 shure I thought my head would explode. dont think it wont one day. Twists and turns 2 bend the head, and rock this complacent whirled. papa dont preach. the subtext in the first one that was drilled into my soul was the text of the second one, and the subtext of the second one was the text of the first. these films were made in different decades, people! the french know their business . . .

When he was done, thousands of words later, it was 3 a.m. For no particular reason, he got up and looked in the refrigerator. Nothing there. Nothing was ever there. He thought about another 7-Eleven run, but then stopped. Too much exertion for one night. Robert then went and got out the journals he had found earlier and took the one from his freshman year, the one he had not gotten to that afternoon. He would spend a few minutes writing down quotes that would establish his sunny disposition for the court, a disposition that he had right up to that tragic day when the Rev. Lester started groping with his lusty paws.

He opened his journal and stood there blinking a couple times. There, on that randomly selected page of the journal, he

read, *I thought my head would explode. dont think it wont one day*
. . . Robert put the journal down, swiveled around, and went
off to bed.

He slept till noon, and when he finally came out of the back,
trying to scratch his back, he staggered over to the cupboards
and got out the cereal he found least intolerable. He thought it
was made out of shredded lawn clippings. He carried it and a
bowl over to the kitchen table and scooted the notepad aside.
He was halfway through the bowl when he noticed the note
from Mys on it.

Love, I thought I would just save you the trouble—we have cer-
tainly talked enough about it! So I just wrote up your statement for
you and took it by the attorney's office to drop it off this morning. We
can still visit with him tomorrow, but he can use it today.

Robert clattered down the stairs in a panic. He burst out onto
the street and stared helplessly both ways. He didn't have a car.
He walked back upstairs.

DINNER WITH THE MITCHELLS

It seems my soul is like a filthy pond,
wherein fish die soon, and frogs live long.
Thomas Fuller

JOHN MITCHELL WAS STEAMED in the abstract. In the concrete world around him at that very moment, to wit, his time at the evening dinner table with his wife and daughter, he was most content. But Chad Lester got to him at the basic worldview level, at the place where theological doctrine and principled animosity intersect in the gut.

On top of that, John had been in puppy love with Michelle Lester in junior high school. But that hadn't been her name then. What was it? Davenport, that was it. He had never asked her out or anything, preferring instead to worship her from afar, usually at a distance of thirty yards or more. The *thought* of Chad Blister just taking one of his early feminine icons off and then treating her that way . . . John was not even sure that he could recall what she looked like back then, and he had never seen her since.

Part of the reason he had not played the role of an aggressive shepherd to Brian Lewis was that he knew that bringing Lewis into the fold would also probably bring in Michelle at some point. And *then* what? Had he ever told Cindi about that junior high crush? Probably. What did it matter? There had been three other crushes, probably that same year. That's what junior high is *for*. And the earth would go around the sun ten entire times before he had finally met Cindi, who, as Puritans go, was as hot as it gets. And, John thought smugly to himself, for those who think that means "not very," he could write a book, although no Christian publisher would ever touch it. She could make him bleed from both his ears, like some very happy kind of parachute accident. John grinned inside his head.

"Careful, these are hot," Cindi said, bending over to place the cheese potato casserole at the head of the table.

John opened and closed his mouth, remembering just in time that Sandy was present. *You bet they are,* John thought. Cindi read his mind and gave him one of her warning looks. After she was seated, they said grace and passed the food gratefully around.

"Anything new about Camel Creek, Daddy?"

"No news today. But I was thinking this morning . . . remember that story that Cherie told us about six years ago? The one about the guest speaker in their college and career group?"

Cindi laughed, "Oh, that was wonderful. Some man named Wilson . . . Tim Wilson, or Jim Wilson, something like that."

"What happened again?" John asked. "I was trying to remember it."

"Somebody in the group suggested a special guest speaker for a week when the designated group facilitator—that's what they call them—was going to be out of town. It was a last minute thing—they didn't do their normal vetting process, and the person who recommended Wilson had only been at the church for a few months. *She* didn't have any notion of the worlds-in-collision she was setting in motion."

"I never heard this one," Sandy said. "What happened?"

"Well, the thing was arranged quickly—Wilson was going to be in town for some other event anyhow, and he didn't know Camel Creek from any other big box church. So he just did what he normally did, which was apparently to teach on confession of sin (acting throughout his presentation as though there really was such a thing as *sin*), and he told everybody that they ought to be doing exactly whatever the Bible says to do. He had to catch a flight right after lunch, and so he never had any idea of the pandemonium he left behind him. About ten people in the class—out of two hundred or so—thought something like, 'You know, that's *right*.' The rest of them were about as indignant as a room full of wet cats."

John chuckled. "That's it. That's what I remember."

"In fact," Cindi continued, "I was just talking to Karen Watson last week, and she told me that she and Tom were part of that small group that wound up leaving because of it. The Watsons and the Craigs. So two of our families eventually wound up at Grace Reformed because of that meltdown."

John's eyebrows went up, which was a significant and bushy event. "I didn't know that part."

"Why were you trying to remember this?" Cindi asked.

"Oh, I just have had Camel Creek on the brain the last few days. Everything I hear reminds me of what they are doing over there. I was looking something up today in Calvin and came across the phrase *confession of sin*. And then I remembered that those words were uttered one time on the actual premises of Camel Creek. But I couldn't remember the story."

"Now John, you aren't thinking *too* much about Camel Creek, are you? You know how it agitates you."

John grinned, somewhat grimly. "But it gives my preaching that secret fire."

"You have also been up at two in the morning with heartburn three times in the last few weeks. I just don't want you . . . you know . . . to get too stressed. I want your blood pressure to do normal, happy things." And Sandy nodded her cheerful agreement with her mom.

John was mildly irritated, not at Cindi, but with that special kind of vaguely aimed irritation that we reserve for ourselves when in the presence of people who are being correct in our direction. And so he did what he always did whenever he felt that way about his dear wife being right, which was to swallow it, say nothing, and show nothing. He knew she was right. He needed a different secret fire pretty darn quick.

A phone in Cindi's handbag, hanging by the door from the kitchen to the garage, chirruped merrily. Cindi left her ice cream on the table and, after a few moments of rummaging around, found it. "Hello?"

Within seconds the pleasant look on her face vanished. "Here," she said, "you need to talk to John." This was not because Cindi did not know how to handle her cousin Cherie, but rather because her husband was better than she was at deciphering code whenever Cherie was hysterical. And Cherie, on the other end, was speaking something like high-volume Navajo under stress.

John listened gravely for a few minutes and then sat bolt upright in his chair. "Lester? Lester is *there?*" The random collections of syllables from Cherie indicated the affirmative. "I'll be right over," John said. He snapped the cell phone shut and handed it back to Cindi.

He got his jacket on, and stood for a moment by the door, waiting for Cindi to warn him about letting Lester get under his skin. But she just kissed him on the cheek. "You are a good pastor," she said.

Cherie's apartment was about ten minutes away when the traffic was light, which it was this evening. By the time John veered off the freeway exit, he had several opening speeches prepared. He wasn't sure which one he was going to use. They were all very fine, and all built on the foundation of the doctrine of total depravity, a doctrine that had been so lucidly formulated by the theologians at the Synod of Dordt in seventeenth-century Holland. Not that he expected Lester to know all that historical theology stuff, but he *did* expect that Lester would still catch the drift. He was going to be civilized about this—he had already dropped the words *worm, cockroach,* and *invertebrate weasel* from his speeches, and yet they all still retained a very robust character.

He pulled up in front of Cherie's apartment and yanked on the emergency brake harder than he usually did. The handle came off in his hand. *Stupid brake.* He walked deliberately up to the door and knocked more softly than he usually did. Self control is one of the fruits of the Spirit. He found himself doing breathing exercises that he and Cindi had learned in a birthing class many years ago.

Within seconds, Cherie pulled the door open. Her hysterics were gone, but her eyes were puffed up and she was sobbing. Her blouse was badly disheveled.

John stepped into the apartment, past the small bathroom that was the first room on the right. The narrow hallway led into a kitchen on the left and a small dining area on the right. It was a screwy apartment. "It'll be all right, Cherie," he said, patting her hand. He led her to a chair in the dining area, where she sat down, still sobbing. "Is Lester still here?" he asked.

She nodded silently.

A male voice came from the living room, located way at the back of the apartment. It really was a screwy layout. "Cherie? Is someone here?" Lester came around the corner and stopped abruptly when he saw John. "What . . .?" he began, and then he saw Cherie and her disheveled clothes.

If John had been paying close attention to Lester's face, he would have seen him go white, the way men do when they see a trap swinging shut on them. But John was not paying attention to Lester's face—he was deciding which of the speeches he was going to launch into. And as for that, it probably didn't matter, because he was going to use them *all*, and it was just a matter of which order they would come in. But still, he wasn't watching Lester closely, who was staring in high indignation at Cherie.

Lester turned to John. "Surely you don't believe . . ."

"What am I supposed to believe?"

"I came over to talk, visit a little, catch up . . . old friends . . ." His sentence rolled to a stop against the wall and just sat there, abandoned.

"He attacked me," Cherie said. "I said no, *no* . . . he wouldn't listen."

Chad Lester was appalled by this dishonesty, as only a dishonest man can be. For those who have never seen this phenomenon in action, he was the kind of man who was entirely unaccustomed to looking at lies from this end of the barrel. He was now counting the rounds in their chambers. He could see their pointed, silvery tips. He licked his lips.

"She . . . she is *lying* . . . we visited a bit . . . she said she was having digestion problems and had to use the restroom. She must have called you from there."

Cherie shook her head violently. "He said he wanted to talk. But after just a few minutes he started pawing me again, *just* like old times. I said *no,* but he insisted. So . . . so I pretended to change my mind and asked to freshen up first. I went to the bathroom and called you."

John went to the phone and picked it up, intending to dial 911. "What are you doing?" Lester asked.

"Calling the cops. What does it look like?"

"No," said Lester and Cherie simultaneously. "Don't do that."

"Why not?" John said, looking at Cherie.

"No cops. I don't want to talk to cops."

Chad said nothing, but was looking immeasurably relieved. He wasn't thinking three chess moves ahead like a man in his position really ought to be doing. Had Cherie set him up this way just to give John Mitchell a chance to give him the un-garbled word? The chances were not likely. In fact it was a long shot of the first order for anyone who thought about it, but Chad Lester in his relief was in no frame of mind to think about it.

John didn't argue, but just put the phone down. He knew from long experience that no one was more obstinate than Cherie when it came to things like this. If he pushed, she would just set her mouth in that odd position of hers, and forty-five minutes later it would be all settled, and the settlement would be what-ever Cherie had decided to do in the first place.

"No cops." John said. "Alright, then. Lester. I have a few things that I think you need to hear, and I most certainly need to say. If you will permit me?"

Lester nodded, not really hearing. He was still rejoicing over the *no-cops* attitude displayed by Cherie. Mitchell-words would be no trouble at all. Lester had a toggle switch in his brain that he used to flip years before whenever he was being lectured by his mother, schoolteacher, or any other superior, and it had enabled him to assume the appropriate demeanor of thought-fulness while being chewed out, and all while his mind was meandering elsewhere. He hadn't used that switch in years—he didn't get chewed out anymore—but he still knew *right* where it was.

John started in, not knowing that his congregation of one had already wandered off, and by the end of the short medley of sermons would be in bed with a nubile someone, far more cooperative than Angela or Cherie.

"The fact that your congregation *wants* you the way you are does not mean that you have any right to be that way. Of course they want you that way—it grants them the right to live how-ever they want and still have a scratch 'n' sniff version of the Christian faith. And that is the secret of your success. Your con-gregation assembles with a good will. Of course they do. The prophet Micah says that if a man prophesies wine and beer, he would be *just* the spokesman for this people. People want what they want, and they heap up teachers for themselves, teachers who will give them what they want. You are just one more ear-tickler in a growing pile of ear-ticklers. How you can . . ."

After the first few minutes, Cherie stopped listening also. It was a dressing-down such as she had never heard, at least since her father had died. The fact that it was addressed to Lester was somewhat gratifying, but still, the whole idea made her un-settled. So she just sat quietly for the ten minutes or so that John unburdened his soul, speaking with accumulating vehemence as he warmed to the topic of Lester's uselessness in the ministry.

He did not get quite as far as to say that Lester was a waste of perfectly good skin, but he came close several times.

Finally, after repeating several phrases unnecessarily (the sermonic equivalent of a blinking fuel gauge), John decided that he had to wrap up. He didn't feel any better. He felt like he had just tried to give a tar baby a bath in vegetable oil. Lester didn't look any cleaner, and John just felt gunked. So John stopped talking and just stared for another moment at Lester.

"Anything to say?" he asked.

Lester came back to the conversation and shook his head without speaking.

"Are you sure no cops?" John asked, looking at Cherie.

"No. No cops." Cherie had settled in her mind—when Lester had first called her that evening—what she was going to do. A story in the media is not subject to rules of evidence, cross-examination, and other such discomfiting things, and the media was the arena in which a slow roast of Lester was already occurring. She would grant a silhouetted interview to Mercedes Hanson—Cherie called her Mercedes, but she was known to Rourke and Bradford as News Babe.

"Alright then," John said. "You can leave now." He jerked his head toward the door. Lester started toward the door, and as he began his exit, he clumsily slipped on a throw rug in the hall between the kitchen and the dining area and lurched heavily into John.

John stepped back quickly without meditating at all on what he should do, and, impelled by primal forces he only understood partially, unleashed a powerful right hook. He had done some amateur boxing in high school, and let us just say that all his old skills had not departed from him. His fist connected with Lester's left eye in a satisfying grinding sound and feel—not at all like the *thwack* of the movies—and Lester straightened up, astonished beyond measure. As soon as he did, John's satisfaction fled from him, and Lester, holding his hand over his eye, departed with a silent and upright dignity, like a butler leaving the drawing room of an English manse.

When the door clicked shut behind him, John just stood silently in the kitchen, and Cherie just sat in the chair. After what seemed like an interminable pause, John finally shook himself and looked down at Cherie.

"Are you going to be okay?" he said kindly.

Cherie nodded, no longer sobbing. She seemed very composed, given what had happened. "I'll be fine," she said. *Picture perfect fine,* she thought.

John sat down on one of the other dining chairs. "Can I pray with you before I go?" he asked.

"Sure," Cherie said and half-smiled. "But are you in any shape to pray?"

"No," John said. "But we still should."

A few moments later, he was walking toward his car. He got the parking brake released more easily than he thought he was going to be able to, started up, put the car in gear, and glided out into the street. Like driving into a thick fog, the ministerial guilt settled in around him.

FREEZING THE LINEBACKERS

Ethics: A Christian holding four aces.
Mark Twain

STEPHANIE NELSON WAS THE LAST of the leadership team to arrive. She closed the door lightly (and quite thoughtfully) behind her and walked through the eddying atmospheric tensions to her seat. At that particular moment, no one was speaking. They had apparently opened in prayer already and had even reached their first impasse. And Stephanie was only three minutes late.

Chad looked extremely sullen, and he may actually have been sullen. But of course the black eye would make him look that way whether he was or not. It was a garish, overdone display, about a quarter of an acre, with deep magenta and black and a few isolated blue stripes. That is what had happened when Pastor John Mitchell had extended the right hand of fellowship forcefully to Chad's left eye. Pastor Mitchell had laid hands on him in a way quite dissimilar to what had happened to Paul and Barnabas at Antioch, when relations between clergymen had been somewhat more amicable. John Mitchell had perhaps missed his calling as an amateur boxer, but he had clearly not missed Chad. Chad, still trying to look dignified, despite the purple affront to others, nodded at Miguel.

"Financial report?"

"Tanking. Giving down 35 percent over the last two weeks, and the trajectory doesn't look promising. This week was significantly worse than last week. Interestingly, attendance is only down 10 percent, which means that people are still coming to watch the show but are sitting on their wallets. This indicates some kind of thought-out plan or clear malevolence on their part." Miguel doodled furiously on the edges of his balance sheet while he was talking.

Bill Turner was on the leadership team because he was a world-class bean counter. His many late hours spent in acquiring this valuable profit-and-loss expertise were a large part of the reason that his wife Mary was currently spending assorted hours in the arms of another man. A country song or two has been written about this kind of thing, and the Arkansas poet who wrote them knows whereof he speaks. Still, Bill knew how to count the beans, and it now appeared plain to him that thirty-five out of one hundred of the beans were missing.

"That's just unacceptable," Bill said.

Chad Lester didn't snarl at him, except on the inside. "We all know it is unacceptable, Bill," Chad's soothing outside voice said, sounding just like the library lady at story time. "The reason we are having this meeting is to determine which plan we will adopt in order to not accept it." *You sexless capon,* he added when safe inside his own thoughts again.

Usually Bill would wither when subjected to this kind of thing, but he was feeling quite secure in his knowledge of the bean ratios, and this was coupled with the fact that Chad Lester was clearly in no position to be the hegemon at this meeting that he usually was. Bill moved in his seat in a way that telegraphed his continued defiance. He didn't actually look under the table for the thirty-five missing beans on the floor, but his body language was as clear as Chad's smooth and polished but sandpapery-anyway response had been. Bill's message was sent, then received, and Chad, appearing as unruffled as a black-eyed master of ceremonies can, looked inscrutably across the table for any other signs of rebellion. It was almost impossible for Chad to run the same kind of disciplined meeting that he used to run, although he was still laboring manfully away. His moral authority was apparently stuck, like an oil-soaked T-shirt down in the sump pump, and this made it hard to control the flooding in this elder-meeting basement of his.

His usual technique had been to control comments and any renegade motions with an imperious glance. Not working well these days, but maybe the shiner was not letting the withering glances all the way out. Part of this was because the previous week he had been the subject of two editorials in the city's major paper, not to mention one (pretty funny) editorial cartoon, and on Wednesday the controversy had gone national when he had achieved the high-water mark of two running jokes on Letterman. Here was a mega-bestselling evangelical author, caught up in a sex scandal. How could he not make it to Letterman? Then somebody took the AP wire, stretched it across the road, and waited for Chad to come around the corner on a motorcycle like some nondescript Nazi in pursuit of somebody important in an old WWII movie. *That* had happened on Thursday.

Chad could see that Bill the eunuch was still unsubdued, and this was unsettling. Bill was almost always the first to go over. In this case, "going over" would mean letting Chad handle it, letting Chad continue to lead, letting Chad show them all the way out. And Bill used to play that role just fine. If Bill had been a local potentate centuries before, and his city was under siege, and he had been told by the randy and imperious besieger to "Surrender all your gold, and let us ravish all your women," Bill would have appeared above the city gates to say something along the lines of "Okay!"

In real life, and not just in the epic simile, Bill had known all about Chad Lester messing around with his wife Mary the year before and had done and said nothing. And Mary knew that *he* knew, and he knew that Mary knew it. And yet the closest he got to open confrontation was the time when he had asked querulously about an overdone lasagna. That conversation had lasted thirty seconds; he ate the lasagna anyway, but boy, there were undercurrents *everywhere*. Bill didn't know about David and Mary, but the point was that it didn't really matter whether he knew anything or not because Bill wouldn't do anything. And yet here was *Bill* showing signs of resistance. Chad knew the meeting was in a perilous state.

Mary Turner looked across the table at David. She arched her eyebrow, which meant in this instance, "Say something." As promising as the sign of incipient feistiness in Bill was to everybody, nobody was counting on him to lead the charge. So David went ahead, clearing his throat first.

"Chad," he began. "We need to do the same kind of thing here that we do with all the challenges and obstacles that we have overcome up to this point, um, here at Camel Creek. We need to run some contingencies, and we need to have a series of decisions made beforehand, based on each one of those, um, contingencies."

Chad looked at him, waiting for the next step. David was not quite ready to take it, at least not without help from elsewhere around the table. He wanted to get Chad's resignation as a mere possibility onto the table, even if only as a potential response to the seventeenth contingency, but it was clear that right now Chad would have to be the one to mention it first. And he was showing no signs of being willing to mention it first.

You know about me with Mary? Chad thought at him across the table. *Well, I know about you and Mary.*

Gotcha, David thought to himself. *I just thought . . . you know, contingencies.*

After the controversy first broke, and the first emergency elder meeting, Pastor Martin had refreshed his own memory with a look at the counseling logs in his office and realized there had indeed been a Robert P. Warner II in his past. Staring at the log, it all started to come back to him. He consequently thought that his verbal participation in this transparent maneuver by David would be . . . premature. David looked at him helplessly, knowing that Michael knew what he was trying to do. *I need a little help here,* David simmered. *Got my reasons,* thought Martin vaguely back. *Maybe we can talk later.*

It was Stephanie who came to everyone's rescue, albeit thoughtlessly and without guile.

"I am sure," she said, "that Chad would be the first to resign for the good of the church, if that were ever to become necessary. When men of integrity are under assault, they always think first of others. If the flock can best be protected by the shepherd departing, I am confident that Chad will be the very first one to make that suggestion. I know I can speak for you in this, Chad, because it is a matter of principle—and you have taught us all very well. And *I* know that if you have not yet done this, it is not yet necessary." At this she bobbed her head perkily like a ponytailed girl in a biscuit commercial from 1957.

Chad looked at her gratefully because she was clearly not interested in his resignation at all. The others looked at her gratefully because she had actually mentioned the r-word, and it was now on the table, linked mysteriously to David's seventeenth contingency. And a few of those others also looked at Stephanie in amazement, realizing for the first time that her innocence was entirely genuine, and that there was actually an attractive woman close to Chad who had no idea of his fornicating ways. No *idea.*

Jeepers, thought Kenneth, an elder hitherto silent. Danielle, who couldn't really do the innocence thing like Stephanie could, rolled her eyes, trying not to be envious. Miguel, who had contingency plans all his own, didn't care. Michael Martin had other things to think about. They all, along with the others, were nevertheless grateful that the mere idea of contingencies had been broached, however obliquely. At some future meeting, it would be possible to refer to Stephanie's "very sad suggestion some days ago." Chad was happy that no one was going to do that at this meeting, and the rest were happy that they were going to do it at a future meeting, perhaps as soon as next week. The two understated sumo wrestlers fell back a few paces, panting.

That out of the way, the meeting turned to other aspects of the issue. Chad spoke after an awkward silence. "As I told you all before, the charge is monstrously false. If we allow charges like this to be leveled, unanswered, then what will the harvest be? I had a good meeting with the legal guys this morning . . ."

By this time, the only people in the room who believed him were Stephanie, who would believe anything, Michael Martin, who knew that Chad didn't do it for reasons he was keeping to himself, and Sharon Atwater in the corner recording minutes, whose reasons had more to do with her instinctive knowledge of the nature of Chad's heterosexuality. And out of those three who believed him, Chad's reiterated denial here was so hollow that two of *them* didn't believe him.

"You're right," said David. "What will the harvest be? In the meantime, we need to do something about the pounding we are taking in the press. Maybe a congregational meeting?"

"No," Chad said. "No congregational meeting. The press would have to be there, and that would just be fat in the fire." Everybody realized that *that* was right at any rate, and fell silent.

/ / / / / /

Chad's sports car roared down the interstate, and he took exit 27A and headed south again. This was his third time around the city, and his automotive excursion reflected his state of mind—only the circles his mind was going in were much tighter, by about a factor of ten. No way out. No way in. No way. He was auguring in. Three miles down that stretch of freeway, he downshifted and pulled off the highway on the next exit ramp he came to, turned right at the light, and headed off down a strip occupied by mobile-home dealers, tattoo parlors, and numerous stores full of retail detritus.

It took about ten minutes to find a liquor store. Chad parked behind the store and walked slowly around to the front. He walked in feeling reasonably confident he would not be recognized. He was in a different part of town, a part of town populated by a demographic that was not really the target group for his ministry. He had long ignored them, and they, for their part of the deal, ignored him back. This part of town had their crazy pastors too, but they mainly operated out of storefronts with names like Knee Deep in Glory Gospel Center. And some of their pastors had tattoos, but these were tattoos that said, "I was in the Navy once, before I met Jesus," instead of the uptown ecclesiastical version that said, "I am desperate to accessorize my iPad."

Anyhow, that, coupled with the black eye, should draw a cloak over this whole business. Secure in his anonymity, Chad walked up and down the cinder-block store's four aisles, putting bottles in his small, blue basket at random. He really had no idea how to go on an alcoholic toot, but was doing fairly well at accumulating the necessary supplies nonetheless. The majority of his selections were based on the bottle looking scary, but he also filled it out with some less scary items—beer and whatnot—to make his venture look more socially responsible, and less like he was laying the groundwork for a major bender.

The clerk, who had seen it all before, knew within the first few minutes that this was a customer laying the groundwork for a major bender. He leaned on the counter and made small talk with Chad as he walked around the store. "Yeah, that's a popular one," he said. "Hard to keep that in stock." Quiet for a moment, he then added thoughtfully, "Nice little punch." A hand up for the novice, the sort of random kindness that helps make the world a better place. But the kindness was wasted on Chad, who thought the clerk was asking about the black eye and quickly changed the subject, asking about the price of a bottle of rum, one with a very grim-looking pirate on the label.

When he was done, Chad walked up to the counter and began emptying the basket. The bottles gradually accumulated next to the register, looking like some architect's rendition of a futurist silver city. When there were a sufficient number of high-octane skyscrapers, some of them with lightning bolts all the way down the sides, Chad dropped a couple hundred dollar bills on the counter. Not a good idea to use the card, Chad thought. This guy doesn't care, but somebody else probably does. "Have a good one," Chad said, gathered up his clinking bags, and walked out. The Hyatt was on the other side of town, and he would circle the city two more times before he came in for his landing.

/ / / / / /

It was Mindy's first week working the check-in desk at the Hyatt. She was a sweet girl, and she looked every bit as sweet as she actually was. Her previous job was in the bookstore at Camel Creek, and she had moved to her new job here reluctantly. She had loved her previous job, but, of course, she was the kind of person who loved everything she did. Now she loved it here.

"Welcome to the Hyatt! How may I help . . . Pastor Lester!" she said. The black eye had obscured recognition for just a moment.

"Hello," he nodded.

She recovered herself. "Checking in for just one night?"

"Yes," he said. Feeling that to be insufficient, he added a lie. "Have an early flight in the morning."

"Your eye . . ." she said. "Are you all right?"

"Yes, yes," he said. "Looks worse than it is. I ran into a cupboard door I left open. Should be more careful, especially when

I'm off in the morning to speak at an important conference." He tried to chuckle knowingly.

"Oh!" she said, returning to the status of perky as anything. "Shall I put you down for a wake-up call?"

"Uh, no, that's all right. I may call down later."

"Okay!" She looked down at the two brown bags he was carrying. "Do you need help with your, um, luggage?"

"No, my bag is in the car," he lied again. *Why did I come here? Oh, that's right.* People would find him if he did this at home. He would wind up naked on the roof if he did this at home. He had no idea how to predict the results of what he was planning. He had a vague idea that throwing up might be involved at some point. The housekeeper would ask about that at home. Chad took his credit card back from her and made his way across the lobby to the elevators, clinking merrily as he went.

Just as the elevators were closing, Mindy's cell phone sang a delicate little tune from her purse in the back. There were no customers, so she went and picked it up. "Hi, Mom!" She was silent for a moment. "Uh-huh. Yes, I can pick that up on my way home . . . Walgreen's should be open. Well, gotta go. On the job . . ." She had heard the sliding doors at the front of the lobby whisk open. "Oh, but you'll never guess who just checked in. Pastor Lester! Yeah, he has a flight in the morning." Mindy heard bags thumping in front of her counter. "Gotta go! Love you!"

On the other end, Stephanie Nelson slowly closed her cell phone. For the first time in a number of years, a thoughtful look came over her face. She was pretty sure Pastor Lester was not scheduled to go anywhere.

Hours later, near midnight, when Mindy's shift only had about fifteen minutes remaining, she heard the sound of shattering glass around the corner. It sounded like it was coming from the bar across the atrium, and when she ran out into the open area to look, she was surprised to see a barstool come flying out of the quiet bar, knocking over the menu sign and clattering to a stop next to a yellow floor buffer and startled janitor. There were signs of what looked like a scuffle in the bar, but maybe not quite a scuffle, and Mindy could not quite make it out. A hotel security man blew past her, running as hard as he could. This kind of thing never happens at the Hyatt, at least that's what the security man was thinking. He was also thinking that he hoped Mindy was watching how brave he was being.

Mindy didn't leave her post, but she kept poking her head around the corner, saying "Oh, dear." Things were very quiet, almost immediately. A short time later, right when her replacement arrived, the hotel security man came back, breathing heavily. Mindy had her purse over her arm, but waited to talk to him. "What happened?" she asked.

The security man, whose name was Keith, was always glad for an excuse to talk to Mindy, and so he stopped and tried to act in the ways a true veteran would. "Oh, it seemed worse than it was. The glass breaking was a wine glass, and that was an accident. And the customer was just frustrated with his deteriorating motor skills, but I think the way he smelled had something to do with that—he smelled like living downwind of three Kentucky bourbon plants—which also contributed to the glass breaking, and so then he kicked the barstool over. The bartender was just trying to calm him down when I got there. I got him back to his room. No blood, no foul."

"I'm glad you got there right away, and that nobody was hurt," Mindy said. "Well, I had better go." Keith swelled with pride at these words of implied praise from her and adjusted his belt accordingly.

If Mindy had remained, she would have heard Keith's continued conversation with her replacement, Stacey, and she would have been astounded beyond all measure. With the information that Keith was about to decant, it would have been impossible for her to not realize that the drunk in the bar was none other than the Rev. Lester. She had only been gone for minutes, and though Keith was already missing Mindy, he was doing what he could to impress Stacey, the replacement, and so he was playing up the fact of the unruly customer's black eye, which he maintained was the size of Rhode Island. "It looked like he had been in a real fight earlier," he said. "I had to be on my toes the whole time, all the way back to the room."

Stacey was trying to figure out a way to communicate something along the lines of "my hero" without sounding too gooby. She liked Keith about as much as Keith liked Mindy, and knew she was a little behind Mindy in a race that Mindy wasn't even in, and so she had to play it cool. So she was silent and just looked on admiringly.

The hotel manager had been working late preparing for a financial visit from corporate, so he was there for the excitement.

He had been talking to the bartender about it, and at that moment walked up to the lovebird and Keith, and said, "Want to know who *that* was?" he said.

"Who?" they both said at the same time.

"That was Chad Lester, minister of the biggest church in our whole damn town. I've got a poker buddy over there, a guy named Bill Turner, who's on their board, I think. I am going to call him in the morning and ask what gives. Why is their holy man over at my hotel, busting up the furniture? Hey? Too late to call now. But he'll get a big laugh out of it."

JUSTICE SCHMUSTICE

*Injustice is censured because the censures are afraid of suffering,
and not from any fear which they have of doing injustice.*

Plato

PROSECUTOR RADAVIC LEANED FORWARD, squeaking his chair
with authoritative mien. His long fingers were splayed, hands
together, fingertip to fingertip, as though a spider were sideways
on a mirror, doing push-ups in an agitated manner. His hair,
just a tad longer than it really ought to have been, was slicked
back on each side, giving the appearance of an attempted comb-
over without actually going for it.

"Tell me that again, Detective Rourke," he said. "I am having
trouble believing my ears."

The ears that were having this particular difficulty stuck out
from the side of his head like a couple of car doors left open
whenever Rourke's wife would unload groceries from the back
seat of her little Toyota, stacking them the way she did in their
short little driveway. "An SUV would be nice sometime, Daniel,"

she would say when he came out to help her bring the groceries in. And Rourke fully intended to fulfill her wish, maybe for Christmas this year. His periodic interviews with Radavic were a little reminder to keep making the necessary financial arrangements. Shaw in the forensics lab had a nice little Bravada he was willing to sell.

There was no reason why Radavic should have told the detectives that his animus toward Lester actually dated back to their time in high school together. Lester, a year behind Radavic, had nevertheless won three speech competitions that Radavic didn't even place in. *And* he lettered in tennis, while Radavic rode the bench for an unimpressive football team. Not only that, but Lester had been the captain of the Mock Trial A squad in the year when they had knocked out their own school's B squad in the state championship—headed up by Radavic. And Lester had, in the closing argument of that particular case, made a very clever joke at Radavic's expense which had brought down the house. *Radavic had a twitch* had played some sort of role in it.

Not only was there no reason why Radavic should have told the detectives any of this, there was no way that he could have. He was present for all of it, but had told those stories to himself over the years in so many new and inventive ways that he did not know that those events had anything to do with his current motivations for anything. Nevertheless, whenever he thought of Lester, the sinews in his neck got tight. And whenever he thought of running for governor, which he knew that Lester had one time talked about doing, the exocrine glands in the back of his mouth would start to water. A certain kind of life always goes back to high school, a fact often overlooked by otherwise insightful biographers. Grown-up life is just a continuation of high school, a fact overlooked by everyone else.

Mike Bradford sat quietly during the interview, renewing his resolve to say nothing whatever during the course of this mini-drama. It was unfolding in detailed conformity to the script that he and Rourke had talked about at their office just before they crossed the street from the police station to come over to the courthouse. *Just uncanny*, thought Bradford. Rourke cleared his throat and tried again.

"I am sure," he said, "that there are some very fine evangelical churches out there, and maybe there are even some big ones. But this isn't one of them. The place is a snake farm. There appear to be all sorts of activities there that would be better conducted under a flat rock in a dismal swamp somewhere. Some sincere people here and there it seems, but they're the ones who are largely clueless. Those there who do have brains—and of those there are more than a few—are running a game that would make a cardinal's mistress envious."

Bradford raised one eyebrow slightly. *Cardinals had mistresses?*

Radavic furrowed his brow in what he thought was a gubernatorial way, a look he had been practicing in the mirror. "So," he said, "the place is, as you call it, a snake farm. And yet, despite this clearheaded and level assessment, your bottom-line recommendation here is that we give it a pass? Help me out here. Is it not part of our sacred *duty* to the public to be clearing out snake farms?"

"I was speaking of the morality of the place, not the legalities. With regard to the legalities, it appears to me that the main issue in all this—the Robert P. Warner angle—really is a trumped-up mess. If Mystic Union is not running a bogus shakedown, I really don't know my business. I think that is why they went the civil lawsuit route to begin with—easier to try the case in the papers, as is happening while we speak. And, as hard as it might be to believe, there may be some foul deeds in the world that were actually not committed by Chad Lester, and it is my view that this is one of them."

Bradford had been nodding at certain key places so that Radavic would not come looking to him to contradict or undermine his senior partner. And yet he did not nod so much that Radavic would feel the need to wheel on him and demand that he defend the position himself along with Rourke. Thus far it appeared to be working. Bradford was not a coward, but he was a careful man. Besides, Rourke was doing great.

The prosecutor did some more push-ups with his splayed fingers, clearly unhappy. After a moment or two of awkward silence, he suddenly said, "Have you checked with any of the other counseling ministers over there? Perhaps this Robert P. is confused about which one he saw." This was not so much a penetrating flash of insight as it was—to use a term popular with clinical psychologists who have studied this kind of thing—a lucky guess. A blind squirrel finds a nut every once in a while.

Rourke nodded carefully. "Yes, we thought of that. We checked the counseling logs of all the ministerial staff. The only one we haven't gotten to yet is Pastor Martin's logs. They had been stored somewhere and misplaced. They asked us to come back in a couple days. His secretary said she had some staff member hunting around in the basement archives, and they should be able to locate it in 'just a matter of time.' We will check back with them on that today."

Of course, what Martin actually had going on was that a friend of Martin's secretary, a young man who was an intermittent coy friend of Martin's, a student at a nearby art academy, was sitting at home in his apartment, copying out a new counseling log for the dates concerned, only with Robert P. conveniently omitted. It was good pay if you could get it. He had nice penmanship and, being an artist, was able to approximate the hand of the regular secretary.

Radavic glowered. He squeaked his chair again. He grimaced and cleared his throat.

"Well," he finally said, "I want you to make a point of checking back in with Martin's office *today*. And get back to me on it. In the meantime, I have to tell you . . . and I mean nothing against you personally by this . . . that I am disappointed. You are policemen, and you are simply doing your job. Your job, as you see it, is to connect the dots, and if a few dots are missing, you believe that it is your duty simply to stop there. I do not. Sometimes you have to add some dots. So as a public servant with a great deal more responsibility entrusted to me, I have to tell you . . . I have a feeling in my gut about this one."

So do I, thought Rourke.

Me too, thought Bradford.

"I am sure that if we keep shaking this, the facts will come tumbling out. Sometimes you have to run ahead."

Yikes, thought Rourke. *Without a shred of evidence . . .*

Crikey, thought Bradford. *Without a shred of evidence . . .*

"After you talk with Martin's office, unless you have positive evidence that indicates that someone other than Lester did this horrible thing, I will probably bring an indictment."

With that, Radavic swiveled his head and looked straight at Rourke with what he thought was a steely, gray-eyed gaze, like in those TV legal-office drama shows, at an especially tense moment when one of the handsome actors rivets another handsome actor with an unshakable and hardened resolve and says, "Dammit, Trevor, this is our *job!*"

We really do need that SUV, thought Rourke.

/ / / / / /

Michelle pulled her gray Beemer into her spacious driveway, waited as the garage door went up, and then pulled into the bay. Shannon and Kimberly both got out of the back seat, stretched, thanked their mom for the bonding time, grabbed their stuff, and headed off to their respective bedrooms.

The phone started ringing just as Michelle walked into the kitchen, carrying her overnight bag. She dropped it on the floor and picked up the phone.

"Brian! Oh, thanks for calling . . . no, we just walked in." She paused for a moment. "No, dinner would be great. I'll tell the girls. They should be okay. I know they have stuff to do. Shall I meet you at South of Texas? Our regular spot? Seven sounds great."

She hung up the phone and dashed up the stairs to freshen up. As much as she didn't want to say so, the weekend of journaling and talking with the girls had done nothing for her at all. The more she wielded her shovel, the bigger the hole seemed to get. And now all she really wanted to do was talk with Brian. And she knew she was going to have to tell him about the divorce settlement sometime. Why not tonight? Still, she didn't really want to.

Brian had been her investment broker, which is how they had gotten acquainted in the first place. He had recommended a local divorce attorney, a friend of his in their office complex, someone who "had real integrity." But Michelle had decided that she actually wanted to go with a firm that used to represent her father back home. The reason for this move was that Chad would know nothing about him or his reputation. And because the lead attorney in that firm—Joe Shattuck, Esq.—spoke with a thick Mississippi accent, this always put urban sophisticates off their guard. Shattuck had made a lot of money that way. At any rate, the plan he had worked out with Michelle had worked, and Michelle had gotten everything she had asked for in the settlement. She had paid handsomely for Shattuck's expertise, but it had clearly paid off completely.

The ramifications of what all this would actually mean for Chad would not become apparent to him until after the divorce was final, when it would be too late, over and done. Chad would not be penniless, by any stretch, but Michelle was walking away with far more than Chad was currently anticipating that she would. His attorneys, some of the aforementioned urban sophisticates, had spent a great deal of time, after their periodic phone conversations with Shattuck, trying unsuccessfully to imitate the way he talked. "Rubes and cornpones are way too easy" was the general sentiment around the firm. After the divorce settlement went into effect, and Shattuck filed a few papers, these same attorneys would have a series of very painful conversations with Chad, with no attempts at mimicry involved at all. Not that they knew about it at the time, but Shattuck had pulled all their shirts up over their heads and rolled all their socks down, creating a little black wool bead around the tops of their expensive Italian shoes. Shattuck, for his part, during a weekly lunch with his partners at a local catfish emporium, was fairly expressive in how he explained what had happened: "Those boys couldn't pour piss out of a boot if the instructions were written on the heel."

Michelle was pleased with how it was going to work out, and the divorce would be final next week. The only thing that troubled her was how she was going to explain it to Brian. He was an honest broker and a really decent sort, and since he would still be handling all her investments after the divorce, he would surely ask some questions about where all the money was coming from. There was no way she could keep it from him—not that she really wanted to—but she was also half-afraid that he would disapprove at some level. Or *something*. She hated the thought of him disapproving . . . but not as much as she hated the thought of Chad getting the best of her. But she would tell Brian tonight.

They were halfway through the dessert before she made her first serious attempt to bring it up. She tapped on the remains of her crème brulee with her spoon. "Brian, there is something we have to talk about . . . something financial."

"Business?" he said. "Mixing romance and business?"

"No, not business details. You can do all that at the office. It's something about the divorce."

Brian reached across the table and took her free hand in his. "Tell me," he said.

And so she laid it all out. She told him about how shrewd Shattuck had been, and how the whole thing was *perfectly* legal, and how furious Chad would be. He would be mostly furious because he took great pride in being a world-class finance *meister,* but a good portion of his anger would be because he had not suspected that Michelle would try to get back at him *that* way. She was still astonished that she had succeeded. The way Shattuck's plan would work would be too tedious to relate, but it concerned a couple of acres of stock options, not to mention their winter getaway home in the Bahamas, both of which Chad had assumed—on the other side of the legal i-dotting—would belong to him. But, as it turned out, they would belong to someone who was actually not him. But tedious or not, Michelle related it all to Brian, who followed her carefully.

"And so I wanted to tell you about it before it all became final. I . . . I wanted to know what you thought of it."

Brian had a hard-to-read look on his face. After a moment, he said, "Look, honey, I don't know what I think of it. I have a hard time feeling sorry for Chad over anything. But obviously, you have some level of concern about it. I don't know. It sounds legal, but I don't know that I would like something like that being done to me. You're asking what I think about the ethics of it, right?"

She nodded, and they both sat quietly for a moment. "Here," he finally said. "Give me a day or so to think about it. Would that be all right?"

Michelle felt curiously let down. "Sure," she said. Then, a second later, "You're not going to talk to Pastor Mitchell about this, are you?"

He said *yes*, and the following quarrel took about twenty minutes. It was a nice restaurant, and so the quarrel stayed subdued and quite civilized. They mostly patched it up near the end, but she didn't go home with him to his apartment. They kissed in the parking lot, somewhat perfunctorily, and went to their separate cars. She pulled onto the freeway in an agitated frame of mind. That was the *only* problem with Brian. Everything else was perfect. Why should he care what this Mitchell character thought? Well, *she* sure didn't.

/ / / / / /

After their session with Radavic, in which Rourke and Bradford learned that the prosecutor's grasp of the elemental principles of justice was tenuous, they found themselves standing outside the courthouse. They waited at the crosswalk for the light to turn, and for a moment no one spoke. Rourke pushed the big flat button on the gray metal pole for a walk signal and then put his hands back in his pockets.

"Bradford," Rourke said, "when we get back to our offices, the first thing I am going to do is write a memo to the prosecutor, following up on our little visit with him. I will make sure that the memo is from the two of us and represents our sentiments exactly. In that memo, I am going to make it clear—in an understated and respectful way—that our recommendation had been to not proceed with an indictment. This will not be done in such a way as to enflame our ambitious friend, but the point will at least be registered. I am sure he will not even notice, but in the cold light of day afterward, our position will be so cogent and clear, and I would be unembarrassed to read about this memo of mine on the front page of *USA Today*. I will e-mail you a copy of the memo, and you will e-mail it back to me a couple times, with some sort of clear approval indicated. We will archive this sentiment in numerous places. I bet reporters, with their freedom of information requests, will have no trouble finding it at all."

Bradford snorted. "Rourke, I do believe that this is an exercise in what a cynical person might call 'covering your tail.'"

Rourke smiled grimly, looking at the sky, which had become agitated during their visit with Radavic. The gray clouds were tumbling over one another, each one trying to get to the front.

"Well, Bradford, what should I say if, looking at a sky like that, I said aloud that I thought I should wear a raincoat, and you said, 'You're just doing that because you think it might rain'? Would an objection of this caliber disturb me? Bradford, it would not unsettle me, not even a little bit. Not even for a moment."

"Ah," Bradford said. "You're telling me that there are times when tails need to be covered."

"You betcher. Nothing else you can do about it when some public servant in authority over you gets his high ambitions all tangled up with moral indignation. *Time for the old raincoat memo*, I says to myself. Remember that Nifong character and the Duke lacrosse players? I had an old friend from the academy who was involved in that one. Boy, was he glad for the old memo move. To this day, he is still able to make the mortgage payments on his house. His wife is happy and I, as an old friend, am also happy."

"Ah," said Bradford. This is what mentoring was all about.

A STEADY BEARING RATE

Injustice is relatively easy to bear; it is justice that hurts.
H. L. Mencken

IN THE U.S. NAVY, a steady bearing rate is not really a happy thing. Since this involves basic physical principles operative all over the globe, it is not a happy thing for other navies either, but the U.S. Navy will work for purposes of illustration. Say that a ship spots another ship 30 degrees off the starboard bow, and let us say the ship is a little bobbing dot on the horizon. Then suppose that some time later, it is still occupying the same place 30 degree-wise, but it is no longer a dot, but rather the size of something significantly bigger than a dot. Then, a half an hour after *that*, if the ship is still right there, 30 degrees off the starboard bow, but this time it is three times bigger and a lot closer *still*, this indicates that unless something changes—and soon—there is going to be a collision and at least three heads on the admiral's desk in the morning.

Some of the characters in our story were not keeping track of the size of the dots.

///////

Mystic Union was nothing if not industrious. Not only did she continue her ordinary herbal sales, in which her dogmatism more than compensated for her lack of expertise, and a demanding slate of midwifery appointments, with no deaths yet, but she also had taken on the equivalent of a full-time job in her advocacy of the Robert P. Warner II situation. Her lover, if he could be called that, wasn't being exactly helpful, because the more energy was expended on the matter of his civil suit against Chad Lester, the more it made him weak and trembly all over. Mystic Union regularly gave him some herbal tea for it, but her concoctions really were a nasty business, and so he just poured it down the sink when she wasn't looking.

She had persuaded the two city papers—one morning edition and one evening—to accept an interview with her instead of with Robert. Those interviews had actually gone quite well, with Mystic Union sharing some lurid details that hadn't really happened. But despite the untruths involved, they nevertheless made good copy, and the editors ate it all up with a spoon, straight out of the carton. One of those editors had read some Derrida in college, and so he was good with the idea of perspectives from every which direction, especially if it made good copy. Mystic Union also, with the natural shrewdness of a born master, knew when to leak and when to go on the record. In one fashion or the other, she kept a steady stream of information flowing to the appropriate news outlets.

Robert P. Warner II wasn't stupid though. He was lazy, he was narcissistic, and he could act like a moron sometimes, and for some reason he thought he knew how to write, but he wasn't stupid. He could see that Mystic Union was going to shoot the moon, and he instinctively knew that his story wasn't built for no moon shooting. And when this small instinctive notion lined up with his inveterate slothfulness, it gave him all the moral authority he needed to go limp and stay that way. He would consistently sleep in till noon or after and walk around their neighborhood for a couple hours, foraging for the kind of food that was not to be had back at the Health Temple. Come to think of it, maybe that had something to do with his lack of cooperation too. If the moon got successfully shot, then there the two of them would be, as wealthy as all get out, but he would still be eating those slabs of tofu.

Robert walked out of the 7-Eleven with an order of cheese-pump nachos, a hot dog, and a couple of packets of those chocolate thingies with a half-life of seventy-five years. He backed out the door, balancing all that processed nutrition along one arm, with a Big Gulp soft drink in the other hand. He walked over to a nearby park and settled with a sigh on the nearest park bench. He could only afford to eat like this because his sister would occasionally send some money. Mystic Union had cut him off a long time ago. Why would a film critic of his caliber have to resort to sneaking around for some decent food? Didn't they feed the critics at Cannes?

But as he ate, he slowly realized the path of least resistance was still to remain for the present at the Health Temple. Mystic Union knew how much she could get out of him, and she didn't push *too* much, so it wasn't at intolerable levels yet. Robert P. ate the hot dog pensively, looking forward to the yellowy-orange nachos.

/ / / / / /

Cherie walked confidently up to the main building of the television station. She had called the day before, gotten through to Mercedes Hanson, and told her that she had a bombshell story to tell about Chad Lester and Camel Creek. She was willing to be interviewed on the record, but anonymously. "You know, the way you guys sometimes interview silhouettes?"

Mercedes jumped at it. "Of *course* we can guarantee you complete anonymity. It is important for the public to know what has been happening here. And we will always protect our sources. The First Amendment guarantees . . . what was that?"

Cherie had asked directions to the station, not being all that interested in the First Amendment. All she wanted to do was get even with Chad, and to do so without taking any responsibility for anything herself. Talking to the police would have probably involved talking about her earlier romps with Chad some years before, in which questions about her cooperation and willingness might naturally have arisen, along with questions about why she stayed at Camel Creek afterward. She had wanted to get back at Chad for years, but there was no real way to do it. But now . . . now, with all these other charges out there . . . now there was blood in the water. She could get her lick in, at little or no cost. Doing it this way, she could just tell her most recent version of the events of the other night, John would feel duty-bound to confirm portions of it if anything did get out, and she did not have to prove anything. All she had to do was tell her story and let the public decide.

So the interview was conducted the next morning, and Cherie felt very good about how it had gone. Mercedes was a deft questioner, one who knew how to look as though she was asking penetrating hardball questions, but who was actually steering the interview straight to the foregone conclusion. Her abilities in this regard gave the phrase *video feed* a whole new meaning.

The last question was a setup for the final appeal: "Why should anyone believe your story?"

"I . . . I guess I am not asking them to." Cherie spoke with a winsome humility. "All I want to do is provide an encouragement to others who may have been in a similar circumstance. Maybe with Chad Lester . . . maybe with someone else." Her voice broke.

"Thank you, for women everywhere," Mercedes said. "Thank you for your courage."

//////

John Mitchell was staring at the screen in disgust. "Courage!" Cindi had just arrived in the living room and was standing behind the couch, drying a roasting pan. She had heard the last part of the interview from the kitchen and came out to watch it with her husband.

"John," she said. "Do you think that's Cherie?"

John Mitchell was slumped on the coach in a posture of strong disapproval. "Yeah, that's Cherie. The first part of the interview you missed was the same story from the other night. But why do *you* think it might be Cherie? They ran her voice through a garble box."

"Just little turns of phrase she used. What are we going to do?"

"Well, this is a queer business. She said nothing about her fling with him a few years ago, which *is* something that would have been easy to prove, if proof were ever necessary. She only talked about the other night. I am starting to think that she set Chad up . . . as much as it pains me to believe that Chad didn't do something grotesque. Maybe she called me as soon as Chad got there . . ."

And maybe John had given Chad a black eye for nothing. Well, there was *that* satisfaction anyway.

"What are you going to do if they call you for corroboration?" Cindi asked. "If she is lying, then that has to be why she called you over."

"They won't call. They already aired the story. And they will only check after the fact if someone challenges the story. And who is going to challenge it now, given that Chad, in the public eye, is up to his neck in precertified guilt? I'll give Cherie this—her timing is impeccable."

"Should we talk to Cherie about it?"

"Probably. Not that it will do any good. But I might have to talk to Chad about that black eye I gave him. But speaking frankly, Cindi my dear, I'm not up to *that* yet. I will need some seasons of incessant prayer . . . that and a couple helpings of your cheese potatoes. What a tangle! Pastoral snarls are like the mercies of God—they are new every morning."

//////

Michelle Lester had gotten over her anger with Brian. He meant well. He was a genuine sweetheart. And for the first time, it occurred to her that she really had no reason to be dubious about any counsel that John Mitchell might give. *That* was a strange thought.

The glimmer of a willingness to have Brian talking to John about her Chad money unfolded into a momentary openness to meeting John sometime to see what Brian saw in him. It went away almost immediately, but still, it had happened. And she was no longer upset with Brian.

But she was still concerned about her girls. Even though their journaling seemed honest enough—and when they talked to her, they said all the right things—she was still worried. Something didn't seem right.

They really needed professional counseling. There was a small battalion of professional counselors at Camel Creek, but she knew the girls would not be open to that. *Icky, gross,* she could hear Kimberly saying. And Shannon would nod.

She flipped anxiously through the yellow pages and came to rest on a small ad for certified counseling services that had a Christian-sounding name. She plopped the phone book on the counter and dialed. The receptionist was cheerful and had some openings for early the following week. When she hung up the phone, the receptionist whistled and took a note into Stefan MacDonald, the counselor. He looked at the note, and *he* whistled. Shannon and Kimberly Lester. Well, imagine that. Stefan had his degree in counseling from Duke and another degree in theology from Westminster Seminary. He was an elder at Grace Reformed and was one of John Mitchell's closest friends.

//////

"Charles Peaborne is a prophet without honor in his own country. Check out his take on all this at savanarola.com."

This was the cryptic comment left at multiple blog sites whenever the Camel Creek reactor-scram meltdown was being discussed, and the comment was left by various posters. There was george@yahoo.com and littlepete@yahoo.com and jojo@yahoo.com. There were a number of others as well, but this would be to belabor the point, because the point of origin for all of them was Charles Peaborne himself. He also tweeted the same message all over tarnation.

There were various levels of praise for Mr. Peaborne from these anonymous admirers, ranging from mildly adulatory to idolatrous. And, for the first two days, they did boost his web traffic a skosh. But after that it was back to the flat brain wave. Charles was on a first-name basis with the guy in tech support for his web stats page, calling him at least three times a day with suggestions on how he ought to check again. Charles also took out a few web ads on various whistleblower sites. But somehow, no one really wanted to click on "Smell the stench of true corruption."

Once you got to the Savanarola website, it was initially impressive, then overwhelming, then odd, and then funny. This was the ranking, depending on whether you spent thirty seconds there, three minutes, ten minutes, or half an hour. The site was jammed full of PDFs of minutes from ancient meetings, PDFs of long-lost memos (mostly from Charles), and PDFs of affidavits (all from Charles and immediate family members). Charles had unique views on what constituted corroboration. He would produce an affidavit saying that he had once told Chad Lester, to his *face*, that if Camel Creek did not repent of its wasteful practice of buying high-grade paper for the copiers, and instead go with the perfectly acceptable middle-grade variety, there would be *consequences*. Then there would be two other affidavits, from his mother and younger brother, testifying that Charles had indeed told them that he had said this to Chad.

It was the middle of the evening, and Charles had just finished uploading a whole new line of what he called "exposure documents." He sat back in his chair in his study at home and stared at the screen, highly pleased.

/ / / / / /

That same night, Miguel Smith was across the state line on one of his periodic forays in search of sexually precocious minors. He always took care to stay away from his hometown in the belief that how he got laid was none of his hometown's business. And unless he traveled afar, the chances were good that word would get *around* in that hometown, and it was possible that his hometown would not take the same lax views on his private affairs that he did.

The internet was a great help in setting up these various liaisons, and the state line was only a few hours away. And so it was that same night that Miguel cruised slowly up to the agreed-upon Holiday Inn Express and saw a long-legged blonde standing by the garbage can outside the main entry, just like she said she would. Her screen name was Tiffany, and she had better be as young as she said she was. She looked like she might be.

The young woman saw his blue-gray Lexus rolling up the drive, recognized it, and sauntered toward the curb. Without missing a beat, she opened the door on the passenger side and hopped in, held up a room key, and said, "Room 106. Just on the other side."

He pulled around to the right, and drove into an empty space right in front of 106. They spent a couple minutes negotiating, agreed on a price, and he gave her the money.

"Well, Tiffany," he said, "it will be a pleasure to . . . meet you."

"Well, actually," she said. "it's Lt. Tiffany." She held up her badge, and at that same moment, a flashlight came on just behind Miguel and focused on the steering wheel.

"Damn," said Miguel.

Lt. Tiffany hopped out, and the voice behind the flashlight said, "May I ask you to get out and step away from the car, sir?"

"Damn," said Miguel. "Okay, though."

But Miguel had contingency plans for everything. The bulk of his money was hidden away in multiple places, and he had resolved some time ago that if he ever got busted—for *anything*—he would behave in such a manner that the authorities would believe that they would all go to their graves without ever again meeting such a cooperative prisoner. He would tell them anything and everything about anybody—except where most of his money was—and he would do it with narrowed gaze, looking for the mother of all plea arrangements. He would spill the first free information before he got an attorney there, and would spill as it suited him thereafter. The confession before his attorney arrived would be for establishing his sincerity in confessing all the rest later. In the car on the way to the station, Miguel decided which confessional track it would be.

Forty-five minutes later, he was sitting in an interrogation room, heavy on the plastic products, from the table to the floor to the chair to the window blinds, and speaking with a heavy-set officer in his forties named Jack, not nearly so attractive as Tiffany had been. Oh, well.

"What do you do?"

"I am the CFO for Camel Creek Community Church."

The man's eyebrows went up. "Camel Creek, eh? You guys get around."

"You've apparently heard about Chad Lester then? Well, this arrest is no doubt God's payback to me for what I have been doing for *him*. I have been issuing checks to a number of his ex-mistresses . . . well, actually, I wasn't able to do that by myself. One of my colleagues, Charles Peaborne, was involved in that part of it too."

The policeman looked slightly panicked. "Look, you have a right to an attorney . . ."

"Oh, I know that," Miguel said, waving his hand. "In fact, I want to call an attorney now. But that doesn't change the fact that I intend to cooperate fully with you guys."

Jack looked pleased, licked his pencil, and wrote down *mistresses, pay off,* and *Charles Peaborne.*

/ / / / / /

Stephanie Nelson looked thoughtfully at the schedule that Sharon Atwater had given her. No plane trips anywhere on it. Chad had been in town for two straight months. She had then double-checked with her daughter. Yes, Chad had *definitely* said that he was catching a plane in the morning. No mistake possible.

Stephanie pursed her lips, highly displeased. She was the kind of woman whose absolute support was freely and completely given, until it gave way like a saturated California hillside. Then it was mostly at the bottom with a car or two underneath. The final event that would cause the hillside to give way might be completely trivial—perhaps a robin landing too heavily—but once the business was underway, well, it was all mostly at the bottom.

Chad had clearly and unmistakably *lied* to her daughter. This was a breach of trust not to be endured. It was clear. It was unambiguous. It was a fat robin. It was obviously time to act.

Fifteen minutes later, Michael Martin looked up from his desk, startled. Stephanie had just blown past his secretary (which was actually a pretty difficult thing to manage) and sat down across from him, her normally pleasant evangelical features fixed, hard, and angry. He gestured magnanimously and just a second too late. "Have a seat," he said.

"Michael," she said. "We have to talk."

He perked up in spite of himself. He had a feeling that this was the kind of anger that would cause her to start confiding. It did not have that "confronting" feel to it at all. In short, she was angry, but not at him. She was angry and wanted his help in being angry.

Okay, he thought. *Sure. Who is it?*

"I feel betrayed by . . . by Chad," she said.

Better and better. "Why is that?" he said, with deep concern.

She told the whole story from beginning to end. Chad had said that he was going to catch a flight in the morning, and he actually wasn't going to. The story didn't take very long. Wasn't much of a story. But Michael was a sympathetic audience. He was not a hard sell. Stephanie was the swing vote on the leadership team, and Michael was there to help her swing away from Chad. But she had already done that by the time she got to Michael's office, and all that remained was for Michael to make a few judicious suggestions on how the next leadership team meeting ought to go.

By the time Stephanie was done talking, Michael had taken it upon himself to schedule an ad hoc leadership team meeting for the following afternoon. Chad wouldn't like it, but it was past time for caring whether Chad would like it. That's why they could have this meeting now. She stood up, greatly relieved, thanked Pastor Martin for his integrity in these dark times, and left. When she was out in the hall, she ran into Bill Turner, who stopped her with an unusual question. "Did you know that Chad was at the Hyatt the other night?"

"Well, actually, I do," she said. "My daughter works there."

"Do you know why?"

"No, I have been wondering that. Nothing wrong with staying at the Hyatt though."

"When you are in your hometown? And you have your own house? I have a friend there who manages that place. He said that Chad was there in order to get falling down snockered."

Stephanie's eyebrows went up. "Snockered?"

"Drunk. He went to the Hyatt to put on his snowsuit and head north. He was on the verge of disorderly and almost busted up their bar there. And my friend said that when they cleaned out his room the next day, they filled up two plastic bins with bottles, a lot of them empty."

"There is a leadership team meeting tomorrow afternoon," Stephanie said. "Michael just scheduled it. Do you think this should be broached . . . there was something I was just talking to Michael about that needs to be mentioned too . . ."

Right then Kenneth, the earthy elder, walked up to the two of them and said, "Guess what?"

Neither Stephanie nor Bill answered, but they both waited expectantly. "Miguel got himself arrested in Memphis. Soliciting an underage prostitute. At least that is what he *thought* he was doing."

Bill whistled through his teeth, and Stephanie, who was surprised at most scandals, wasn't surprised at this one. They both shook their heads, looking at the tile floor.

"But of greater interest," Kenneth went on, "is the fact that Miguel has opened the floodgates of information for the authorities and is talking a lot about Chad."

"How do you know all this?" Bill asked.

"Miguel's attorney called me. Miguel wants us all to know that he has come to the conviction that confession is good for the soul."

Stephanie looked at Bill. "Is there any way we can move the leadership team meeting to the morning?"

/ / / / / /

The leadership team assembled the next morning, first thing, eight o'clock on the dot. Chad was resigned to the inevitable, but was in a combative mood anyway. No sense letting anybody know he was resigned to the inevitable.

They were all initially prepared to let Chad fall on his sword in an honorable way. The raw numbers should be enough. So the meeting began with a financial report, which Bill Turner had prepared for them, the bottom line of which looked like somebody had been spraying it with Roundup. The initial tone was sad—"this can't continue," "untenable," "not realistic," were words and phrases that filled the room. They all gave abundant cues for Chad to pick up on, and they all knew that Chad knew they wanted him to resign. *No*, he thought. *We insist*, they thought back in reply. They all sat quiet for a minute, like Job's comforters after Job had failed to take responsibility for the economic disaster that was befalling them all. Not like Oedipus, who was a real team player. Oedipus would admit to *anything*. Chad was just sitting there. Look at the *numbers*, man.

"I am not going to offer my resignation over anything so worldly as offering receipts," Chad said. "You can vote on my removal if you wish, but I am not going to make it easy for you."

"It is not just the offering receipts. That was just so that we could keep this from descending to personalities," Kenneth said.

"What else is there?"

"You getting drunk at the Hyatt," Bill Turner said.

"I was under a lot of stress. Whatever happened to grace? Wouldn't you get drunk?"

"Not at the Hyatt," Kenneth responded.

Stephanie shushed Kenneth. "Chad, it's over. Miguel has told the police, and us, about all the women and your hush fund. Bill has been going over the books and has found a number of irregularities that you had to know about. You lied to my daughter Mindy about going out of town. And Mary here says that just last month you made unwanted sexual advancements toward her. She has been beside herself, not knowing what to do."

Mary nodded, looking down at the table to avoid eye contact with Chad.

Bill, emboldened, came out to place the capstone. "And we got a note in the offering box this last Sunday telling us that your black eye was given to you by another minister, when he found you in a compromising position with a relative. How *did* you get your black eye?"

Chad spread out his hands. "Just vote," he said.

ENOUGH COURTHOUSE HISTRIONICS

FOR THREE PERRY MASON EPISODES

> *Some circumstantial evidence is very strong,*
> *as when you find a trout in the milk.*
> Henry David Thoreau

MERCEDES HANSON HAD ALWAYS BELIEVED in swinging for the fence. If she was ever to break out of this local news market, she needed to do something *spectacular,* and she was always on the lookout for what that might be. Every story was reviewed by her with this consideration in mind. She was competent, hard-driving, and ambitious, which successfully grouped her in with about three million other blonde local news reporters. She had never heard the term News Babe applied to her, but it almost certainly would not have bothered her if she had. She believed in swinging for the fence, and that meant using *everything* you had. No harm if other people noticed some of what you had.

The court date for the civil trial had been set for the third Tuesday of the month. The months leading up to this point had seen all sorts of motions and countermotions, but this was the first time that everybody was going to be in the courtroom together. Mercedes had succeeded, through flattery, cajoling, and smashmouth negotiations, in securing a very brief interview with Chad Lester at the courthouse just fifteen minutes before he was to appear in the courtroom. She had had the room reserved and secured, and she had her people confirm and reconfirm with Lester's office in the weeks leading up to the interview. At the beginning, it was just going to be a regular interview, but as the date approached, an idea began to form in her mind, and by the week of the court date, she was resolved on what she was going to do. Nothing like a little extra sensationalism in the midst of an already sensational trial. It was a national story already, so why not? She had been in the corridor outside their reserved room many times, and whenever court was in session, it was always crowded. More than crowded enough.

The court time was at 10:00 a.m., and Mercedes was there with her crew at 9:30. There were two connected rooms reserved for them. The first room was small, and that was where she intended to put her plan into action. The second room sat empty, and the only significant thing about it was a door that Mercedes had somehow overlooked, a door that emptied out into another corridor. She had set the camera crew up in the corridor outside the first room so that she could do her preliminary intro and set the stage for what was to come.

Chad Lester had arrived, right on time, at quarter till. He seemed to her to be a pasty, sickly white. Mercedes greeted him and opened the door for him. "I have to finish the setup shot here. We'll be right in. Second room . . . right, go through to the second room."

He disappeared into the door, and Mercedes turned to her cameraman. "Get that?" she asked. He nodded. "Great visual," he said.

Mercedes turned back to the camera, microphone held at the ready. "And so we come to a critical day in a long and distinguished ministerial career. Will this be a day of vindication . . . or of something else?" With that, and with a dramatic flourish, she turned and went inside the door. Her cameraman had been instructed to wait for a few minutes, but he had not known why. News Babe had her quirks. But who didn't?

When the door of the first room closed behind her, Mercedes leaned back against it and took a few deep breaths. Then, without a qualm or a second thought, she put the microphone down, reached up and tore the front of her blouse, pulled herself askew, and then reached up and disheveled her hair. She picked up the microphone, slowly counted to thirty, and lurched back out the door again. She fell out the door and halfway out of her blouse, plainly looking as though she had just escaped from groping clutches. Her cameraman jumped.

"Mercedes!" He started to put the camera down, but she motioned at him fiercely. "The story first," she blurted in a hoarse whisper. She stood upright, pulled her blouse together, lifted her microphone, and in a voice that was barely steady, began to report the story.

"Unbelievably," she said, "this man, Chad Lester, on trial here for sexual misconduct, was unable to control himself even . . . even on the threshold of judgment." She choked up for a moment. "Excuse me," she said after a moment. She hadn't done this well since her supreme moment in a high school production of *The Glass Menagerie.* Everything goes back to high school. Tears ran down her cheeks. Her eye makeup was seriously blurred, and she looked out the twin smudges at the camera.

Staring at this very spectacle on the screen, John Mitchell told Cindi, who was standing behind him, that News Babe looked like a sensuous and emotionally worked-up raccoon.

/ / / / / /

Chad Lester walked into the first room, stopped for just a moment, and then into the second room. He had been afraid of being late, so he had not stopped at the men's room on the way in. But that woman was still out in the hallway, blowing introductory smoke for the viewing public. He put his briefcase in the middle of the table so she would know that he would be back in a minute, and as he stepped toward the back door, a bailiff stuck his head through it. "Rev. Lester?" the man said. "Glad I caught you . . ."

Lester walked right past him. "We can talk as we walk," he said. "Know where a men's room is?"

"Right this way," the bailiff said. There was a men's room just down the hall, or so he thought. It turned out to be one hall after that. A few moments later, Chad was standing at the urinal and told the bailiff to proceed with his mission. "Excuse me, Rev. Lester," the bailiff said, starting over at the beginning.

Chad nodded and almost said, "Just call me Chad," but stopped himself.

"I was told to get word to you and your attorneys that there has been a problem with the ventilation in Courtroom A, where we were scheduled. We had to move to the other side of the courthouse, down to the old courtroom. It'll take a few minutes to get there. I'd be happy to show you the way. I already caught your attorneys at the main entrance."

"Thanks. Thank you," Chad said. He was relieved that he had an excuse for skipping out on the interview with Mercedes. They went out into the corridor, and Chad quickly popped back into the interview room to grab his briefcase—no sign of Mercedes yet—and popped out again. He and the bailiff headed down the corridor and then turned left, a route that would take them right past where Mercedes was standing, blowsy and disheveled, and astonishing the greater metropolitan area with her story. And her remarkable story *was* going to go national, but not in the way she had hoped. She was telling quite a lurid tale.

"When did this happen?" someone in the crowd cried out.

"Just seconds ago," she barely managed to reply. "Just now."

With that reply there was a commotion in the hallway to her right, as the crowd stepped aside to let Chad and the bailiff walk by. Mercedes' cameraman, in fascinated horror, panned over to where Lester was walking with a uniformed official, and then back to his former boss, standing, completely flustered, in front of the doorway.

A cop who was part of the crowd, and who had been carried away by Mercedes' story, stepped forward to take Chad into custody. Chad was just standing there with a serene look on his face. He had started to have the feeling that this was going to be his day. The bailiff leaned forward and whispered in the cop's ear. They talked back and forth for a minute like a couple of refs right after a bad call in a championship game involving fourth down and inches. The bailiff whispered again. "I've been with him the *entire* time."

A voice from the back of the crowd called out to the bailiff, "How long you been with Lester?" The question was from a shrewd observer of the human condition, quicker on the uptake than the cop currently was. The bailiff's brow furrowed. "Five minutes. Why?" He would not get an answer to that question until that evening when he saw himself on the news. Mercedes licked her lips, thinking furiously. "Don't," said her cameraman. "I'm turning this damn thing off now."

In some ways, even though the board of Camel Creek had finally dismissed him the previous week, this day at the courthouse was going to be all Chad's. With a little perspective, letting him go had made sense. Innocence or no innocence, the precipitous drop in offering totals Sunday after Sunday had a way of communicating a nonnegotiable vote of "no confidence." And the leadership team had inside knowledge that wasn't in the papers yet, and some of which, with him gone, might not ever make it into the papers. So *that* meeting had been what some might call "a sociological event." His life was now officially in shambles, and he would have a lot of debris to sort through later on. But not very much of that debris was going to be falling out of the sky on *this* day.

Chad walked into the courtroom and made his way up to the front table with a couple minutes to spare. His attorneys had gotten the word about the switch and were there ahead of him. On the other side, Robert P. Warner II was seated, head down, staring at the table. He was depressed. He didn't have a good feeling about any of this. Mystic Union had spent a couple hours that morning talking him into a suitable frame of mind, and even then it was touch and go. She was seated in the front row, right behind Robert P., sitting at the ready in case she had to encourage him with an emotional rubber hose again. Their cause was in a parlous state.

Robert P. Warner II took three deep breaths and then sat up straight. A man's gotta do what a man's gotta do. He then looked over in Chad's direction for the first time, blanched, turned white, then ashen, and then he blanched again. He tugged furiously on his attorney's arm. "Who's that?" he hissed.

"What do you mean, 'who's that?' That's Lester," the attorney said. If Robert P. had been following his own story in the newspapers, he would have seen Lester plenty of times. But he had been consumed with sleeping and blogging and watching serious French jiggle art and had no time for the case. The case wearied his soul. Mystic Union had followed everything scrupulously, but of course it did not matter that *she* knew what Lester actually looked like. It made, as the fellow once said, no never mind.

Robert P. Warner II swiveled in his seat and looked at Mystic Union in desperation. She had been expecting this look of desperation, but didn't know that this time there was actually an objective basis for it. Nevertheless, she was prepared with soothing encouragements.

But Robert was not suffering here from his general malaise, but rather with the sure and certain knowledge that the man they were suing for molesting him years before—not that Robert had minded it, actually—was not the man who had actually done it. His eyes were wide open, filled with panic, as well as with a sure and certain knowledge of impending doom. There was no way they were going to win this case before, and now there was *really* no way they were going to win it. Same as before, only worse. But when he turned to whisper the problem to Mystic Union, his eyes happened to fall on a familiar face in the back row of the courtroom. There had been no way that Michael Martin could avoid coming to support Chad, and so he had to run the risk of being recognized. But he had taken care to slip into the way back. But Warner's eye fell on him there, as the fates had decreed, and Warner suddenly realized what must have happened. Maybe Camel Creek had more than one pastor! And there his molester was, sitting way the heck at the wrong end of the courtroom. Warner looked away for a moment in consternation, and when he looked back, that seat was empty. Had he imagined it? Doubts flooded over him from one direction, and panic from the other—he was caught in a tsunami crossfire.

Instead of telling his attorney about it, Robert P. Warner II stood slowly to his feet. Mystic Union was gesturing furiously at him, but he ignored her. Throwing his head back, he pointed to Chad and wailed. The courtroom fell silent and listened to Warner, keening and howling and muttering furiously at the ceiling. At first the noise was unintelligible, but after a time, people began to realize that he was saying, over and over again, "That's not him! That's not the one!" This went on for a couple minutes. The judge didn't gavel him to shut up because nothing was in session yet. Everybody just stared, fascinated. And then, as if in response to someone throwing a big breaker somewhere, Robert P. Warner II slumped, shumped, and fell to the floor. He there assumed the demeanor and outlook of a beanbag chair and ceased cooperating with the world.

After ten minutes of pandemonium all around him, furious whispering between attorneys, two conferences with the judge, and ineffectual attempts by Mystic Union to get him to sit up, Robert P. quit saying, "That's not him! That's not the one!" and started saying, "Drop it, *drop* it!" Finally, one of his attorneys stood up, shrugged, and walked over to Chad's table and said, "We are going to withdraw our suit." He then walked over to the judge and told him the same thing. The judge told the bailiffs to get a medical spatula crew, scrape Mr. Warner off the floor of his courtroom, and take him somewhere else.

Chad stood up, ran his hands through his hair, and whistled.

/ / / / / /

Bradford heard about the Warner meltdown from a detective friend who had been there. He could barely understand the story because his friend was wheezing so much, but when he did get it, he muttered *golly* under his breath and said, "Excuse me." He took off at a run, back to the other side of the courthouse. Radavic was not to be denied and had thought that it was his bounden duty to file a criminal indictment that very same day. He was furious about all the column inches that had been going to the civil trial in the weeks leading up to it—although he didn't exactly express it to himself that way, of course—and he determined to do the right thing and bring an indictment. It would be a *principled* stand, and that is all he could or would say about it.

He had a small stack of manila folders under his arm, and he was wending his way to Courtroom B. He was about to go in when Bradford came tearing around the corner, slammed into a wall, and then dashed the remaining twenty yards. Bradford slid to a stop alongside the prosecutor, gasped, "Thank *God*," and then put his hands on his knees to catch his breath.

"Bradford . . ." Radavic said.

"Yes, sir," Bradford said and stood upright. "Thank God you haven't filed anything yet."

"Bradford, I am not going to listen to any more of this crap. Rourke's memo bordered on professional impertinence, but I let it go. Sometimes you simply have to do the right thing."

"But sir, there is something else that has just happened, something you have to take into account. I ran . . ."

"That's enough, Bradford. Not another *word.*"

"Yes, sir." Bradford watched in fascination as Radavic pulled open the thick wooden courtroom door and walked in, the embodiment of civic duty. After the glory subsided somewhat, three reporters followed him in. Since it was simply the first procedural move, Radavic would only be in there for ten minutes or so. Bradford leaned against the far wall, hoping that he would be able to get a sensible word in afterward. But no such luck. Radavic burst forth out of the courtroom at right about the ten-minute mark, glared at Bradford, and strode purposefully toward the main entrance of the courthouse. Bradford followed him at a respectful distance, keeping well clear of the cloud of righteous indignation.

Radavic hit the bar for the main courthouse door with a decisive clatter, and he made it three steps past the door before he stopped abruptly. There, out in front of him, on the courthouse steps, was *Lester* talking to a battery of reporters. He was subdued, but was speaking in terms of quiet vindication. "Yes, yes, it does feel good . . ." he was saying. Radavic couldn't quite catch what he was saying, but Bradford could see the prosecutor's neck get bigger. He had never seen a neck so full of righteousness.

The prosecutor walked slowly up to the cluster of reporters, brimming with news that would astonish them all, and which would then give them the opportunity to astonish Radavic even more about two minutes after that. The microphones were all sticking out invitingly, and Lester and Radavic were standing about five feet apart—like a couple of loudmouth heavyweights at a pay-per-view weigh-in.

"Whatever the Rev. Lester has been telling you about the civil case," Radavic began, "it may interest all of you to know that I have just filed a criminal indictment against the good reverend for the statutory rape of Robert P. Warner . . ."

He would have gone on, but all the reporters gasped, three of them took a step or two backward, and one of the cameramen fell down.

Radavic looked back and forth. "What? What?" he asked.

"It was like watching a helicopter trying to land sideways," Bradford told Rourke later. "I didn't *want* to watch. It felt more than a little creepy. But I had to. I have never been so near such a cringeworthy event, not even close. But when I thought about all those prophylactic memos we sent back and forth about thirteen times, I felt positively spiritual. The wife has been asking, and I think I am going to take her to church."

/ / / / / /

Rourke had been present at the Warner saga, but only because he was looking for Charles Peaborne, and he thought for sure that he would be there. At least that is where Peaborne had said he would be on one of his latest "rip the cover off" blog posts.

Savonarola.com had really taken off—there had been fifty-seven hits there just yesterday. One of them had been Rourke, seeing if Peaborne was planning on attending the opening ceremonies for the downfall of his nemesis, Lester. He was, and so Rourke was there waiting for him afterward.

Rourke was doing that because he had some questions he needed to ask Charles Peaborne. The investigator in Memphis, who had arrested Miguel Smith and done the initial interrogation, had called Rourke to let him know that Smith had fingered Peaborne as the one who had been cutting all the checks to Lester's ex-mistresses. This had been done because Smith had vowed to himself, years before, that if anything bad ever happened to him, taking him out of his cushy position at Camel Creek, one of the first things he would do would be to confess to his involvement in covering up for Lester, and to do so in a way that would implicate Peaborne, right up to the top of his pencil neck. He could not *abide* that man. There had been a six-month controversy over which *toner* cartridges to buy for the church. It had been the easiest thing in the world to arrange the checks in such a way that Peaborne would not know what he was signing. And Peaborne did not know anything about all this, although Rourke was about to bring him abreast.

Rourke walked up to him in the foyer outside the courtroom and tapped him on the shoulder. "Excuse me, Mr. Peaborne? Detective Rourke." Rourke extended his hand and shook the hand of a somewhat startled man. "Do you have a moment for me to ask you a few questions?"

IN WHICH SOME PEOPLE

LEARN THE WRONG LIFE LESSONS

Ephraim is a cake half turned.
Hosea vii.viii

MICHAEL MARTIN WALKED OUT of the meeting of the leadership team shaking his head in amazement. The vote to call him as the new senior pastor of Camel Creek had been unanimous—no dissension, no hesitations whatever. Michael did not have the same gifts that Chad did, but at the same time, he was certainly in the same league. He was professional, cut, chiseled. His slacks had a crease in them that could cut weeds if he walked through a field of tall grass, not that he did this very often. His one idiosyncratic feature was that he always looked like he was chewing beef jerky whenever he talked, but most people who even noticed it thought it made him look masculine in that jaw-jutty way that you see in Eddie Bauer catalogs.

The call was effective almost immediately, and Michael was invited to "share" his inaugural message the Sunday after next.

The reason for the delay was that the leadership team wanted the extra time to run an ad campaign so that they could start this new era off with a bang. The church leadership was prepared to spend a *great* deal of money in order to market the "under new management" theme, and the ad boys in the basement were all over it. Their ads extolling the virtues of flexibility in changing times, adaptability in the face of difficulties, and going-with-the-flowness in the event that your church was ever caught in a flash flood of scandal, were ads that were hip, ironic, self-effacing, detached, and exuded a coolness unto death. The team had pulled a couple of all-nighters, and they now had in hand a flurry of ads that were calculated to bring all the straying sheep back home again. And, it must be said, they knew their business, provided it is assumed that the shepherd's crook can take the form of a PR blitz.

During the scandal, before Chad had accepted the pressure to resign, these graphics impresarios had been just so many advertising hounds locked in the kennels of indecision, with the raccoons of market share running through the woods pretty much as they pleased. It had been a genuine trial for them all. But now, with the resignation in hand, the leadership knew what direction they were going, and the woods were soon filled with the sounds of their baying.

And they did know their business. Camel Creek was about to come roaring back—on all eight cylinders—into the life of their community. Those members who had left had taken their stand for principle, kind of, and their brief exile among all the other area churches had reminded them how much they didn't like the few remaining traditional services out there. And on top of that, neither did they like the wannabe contemporary services with congregations under two hundred, because the drummer was almost always lousy, and the bass player pathetic, largely for size-of-gene-pool reasons. So pretty much all the Camel Creek diaspora were ready to be talked into coming back. They were already checking the newspapers for the long-anticipated ads. They weren't really looking for repentance; postmodern irony would do.

When the leadership team extended the invitation to Michael, they also asked him what he thought his message was likely to be. He had seen their invitation to become the senior pastor coming, and so he was ready with his answer. "I would want," he said, "to speak on 'Integrity and Healing.'" A number of heads bobbed up and down around the table. Encouraged, he expanded his little sermonic trailer for them.

"We must never allow integrity to become the enemy of healing. We must never allow healing to become the enemy of integrity. Only in this way can our church recover its footing, its love, and its missional zeal."

This was not really supposed to mean anything in particular, but the elders were not about to press him on it. All they wanted was for smooth words to flow over them (and everybody else in the audience) like molten butterscotch, and it was looking as though they were going to get everything they were paying for, which was quite a bit of butterscotch.

Martin had been far more discreet about his amours than Chad had been, and speaking quantitatively, if illegitimate dalliances were corn, his Nebraskan combine had not cut so wide a swath, and this meant that many on the leadership team did not even know that they were getting a minister like unto Chad. They most certainly did not know that they were getting the actual fondler of Robert P. himself, but all of that did not come out until quite a few years later. Michael did eventually blow up one day, while pastoring another church in quite another city and state, which is neither here nor there. His ten-year tenure at Camel Creek was serene and placid—idyllic conditions for water skiing, which he most certainly did.

The ad boys did their magic, the team in the financial department wrote checks to media outlets like crazy, and when the Sunday morning in question rolled around, the place was packed like the local college gym would be if some cowtown university inexplicably made the Sweet 16 one year. The atmosphere was as electric as a gathering this mellow could be, with everyone there prepared to get the full neck massage. Maybe *electric* is the wrong word. *Expectant,* that's it.

"Integrity. Integrity and healing. Healing. Healing and integrity," Michael began. The congregation settled comfortably down in their theater seats. *Aaaaaahhhhhh.*

/ / / / / /

Johnny Quinn was sitting with Brandy in the upper section of the auditorium, near the back row. It was ten minutes after the close of Michael Martin's address, and Johnny was still reeling. *Integrity,* he thought. *Healing,* he thought. *Both of them together,* he thought. Brandy sat quietly by him. She could tell that great forces were contending with one another in his soul.

"Wow," he finally said aloud.

"Yeah," she said. "Double wow on me too."

"What a blessing," he said.

"Yeah," she said.

"This is a God thing."

"I agree, Johnny." She nodded—pretty, simple, innocent.

And with her acknowledgment that it was a God thing, it suddenly dawned on Johnny that this was the time he needed to do that *other* God thing. He needed to ask Brandy to marry him. After that police officer had exhorted him about this during his brief foray into pastoral ministrations, Johnny had accepted this course of action as the inevitable will of God. But he had still needed to make the math work, in order to figure out how to pay for a larger apartment and all that other stuff. He hadn't been able to do that. But here . . . clearly, Pastor Martin had delivered a message that was a *God* thing. And if one God thing had happened here in the auditorium, just a few moments ago, why not another God thing? Why the heck *not?* There was no one around them.

"Brandy," he said. "Will you marry me?"

She was startled, but smiled widely. She had a beautiful smile. "Johnny! Of course I will."

He extended his hand, and she put her hand in his. "I don't have a ring yet. We can go shopping for one tomorrow." She nodded happily and then leaned over and kissed him. They got up, holding hands, and walked slowly down the aisle, turned left, and headed out toward the escalators. They chatted happily as they glided down toward the first level. When they got to the bottom, they started to work their way outside. The lobby area was still quite crowded.

Before they got to the doors, Stephanie Nelson saw them from across the way and called out, "Johnny! Johnny Quinn!" Johnny thought he heard someone calling, and so he stopped, puzzled. Stephanie wound her way through the crowd, came up from behind him, and tapped him on the shoulder. Johnny turned around, still in the pleasant glow of the great faith step he had taken. He was still nervous about it, but was certain he was doing the God thing.

"Johnny, the leadership team asked me to talk with you. Dennis Johnston has decided to move on—he has taken a position in Illinois at Sandlefoot. The elders asked me to ask you if you would be interested in taking his place as our lead youth minister."

Johnny's eyes widened. This was a leapfrog promotion over a number of others that he would certainly have thought would have been asked first. And he was aware of how much Dennis had been hauling down. He could afford Brandy now. Brandy was beaming at him, really proud. "I . . . I would be honored," Johnny finally said.

Dennis had decided to head for the tall grass because he had once been involved in an unwitting *ménage a trois* with Michael Martin and one Sandy Duncan, a character of some note and a disc jockey over at the KING radio station. When Martin had been chosen to replace Lester, Dennis thought that getting while the getting was good would seem to be the voice of prudence, before a day of real reckoning came down upon them all. "Fire on the mountain, run, boys, run" about sums up his feelings on the matter. Camel Creek appeared to have some kind of reverse mojo going, and Sandlefoot had been after him to join their team for some time now. This was something of a miscalculation on his part because Camel Creek was actually entering into its golden decade, and Michael Martin did not receive his reap-what-you-sow comeuppance until after he became the senior pastor at another church entirely—Sandlefoot Community, come to think of it.

After Stephanie had offered Johnny her congratulations and told him to check in with her at her office tomorrow to work out the details of his work agreement—"which will be *more* than acceptable, I can assure you"—she retreated back into the diminishing crowd.

Johnny and Brandy stood, staring at each other. "A God thing," they both said at the same time and then laughed. "Now I can afford that ring I'm getting you," Johnny said. They were both thrilled and delighted and walked out through the doors leaning into one another. They had a short engagement, just two months long, and they only messed up one time during that whole engagement.

// / / / /

Sharon Atwater had decided to take the package they offered her. It would have been insane not to. Michael Martin wanted to start the whole senior pastor operation over from scratch and remove, delicately, as many members of the old office guard as he could. The fewer people from the Chad days, the better he liked it. The subject had been broached with Sharon with great professional sensitivity, and Sharon had responded with a corresponding professionalism. "Oh, I would love to move on," she had said. "I just can't afford it. I have to work at least a couple more years before I could move back to Tennessee. I have been planning to go live with my mother, but I would want to help her, not be a drain on her . . ."

Some discrete calculations had been made about what Sharon could likely save up over a couple years, both in her retirement package and elsewhere, and she was offered a severance package that it would have been criminal negligence to refuse. The added benefit of getting away from the gravitational pull of Camel Creek was compelling to her as well.

And so it was that Sharon was busy clearing out her desk and sorting out the office files, preparing them for her replacement, a one Misti Cooper. Misti was competent, sweet, and a quick study. She was also cute and virginal, and made the kind of visual first-impression statement that Michael thought most necessary to make during these, alas, cynical times. During their two-week transition, Misti would come in during the mornings, and Sharon would check her out on all the various office procedures. In the afternoons, Sharon would go through all the files and decide what could go in the archives, what could be thrown away, and what she should keep. She had a few personal files of her own here and there, and she was now seated in her rolling office chair in front of one of them.

Many years before, she had been in the second row of that infamous class taught by the equally infamous Jim Wilson. The talk had been on confession of sin, and the effect of it had been the equivalent of dropping a hand grenade in your average living room goldfish bowl. Sharon had (for some reason) saved the handouts from that meeting and was sitting awkwardly in her chair now, holding the manila folder in her hand, trying to figure out why she had done that. There was something that looked like a confession-of-sin graph and another handout with a bunch of Bible verses all over it. Sharon squinted to make out the marginalia she had scribbled on the papers at the time. *Damn fool* was one comment. *Superficial idiot* was another. She had been among the displeased in that class, but now a wave of sadness swept over her.

At that time, she had been in love with Chad and had hoped his wandering attention would return to her. But it never had, and the verses no longer seemed insane to her, the way they once had. She sat there for fifteen minutes, trying to make up her mind about the three sheets of tattered paper. Throw it away or not? Suddenly the phone rang, and Sharon got up without dropping the papers in the trash can she had dragged over. When she picked up the phone, she placed them carefully in the box for moving stuff that was sitting on her desk. It did not seem like an important act at the time, but those papers would make even more sense in Tennessee.

//////

Charles Peaborne had literally wet his pants when it first dawned on him what Miguel had done to him. He was not a brave man in the best of circumstances, and the only time he could be prevailed upon to put up any kind of a show of courage at all was when the stakes were remarkably low—something other parties to the conflict would unlikely be willing to fight over. Paper clips, toner cartridges, grades of copier paper were the way to go. Everyone else would always just roll their eyes at some point, and after a certain amount of time and energy was expended on the quarrel, would just capitulate so that Peaborne would go expend his energetic and remarkable abilities of *focus* elsewhere. This he would usually do, and a brief respite for the victim of his dudgeon would be earned thereby.

By this means, Peaborne had come to fancy himself a natural member of the warrior caste. He had been on a retreat once where he sat naked in a little teepee, pouring water on hot rocks, and this had helped to release his inner wildness. He talked about that experience frequently as though he had been one of the six hundred who had ridden into the valley of death. In short, he was a coward who had absolutely no idea that this was what he was. He was an irritating midge that some could occasionally be persuaded to brush at absently, or blow half-heartedly off their lip, but he was not the formidable foe that he fancied himself to be.

Except that there had been that one time when he actually got to Miguel, and the level of irritation was such that it prompted some level of action after Charles Peaborne had disappeared around the corner. *That* didn't usually happen. But Miguel determined that he would not get mad, but rather just get even, and so he had quietly adjusted the bookkeeping setup. The arrangement needed an overhaul anyway, but Miguel tweaked it, making sure that if any women were getting checks from Camel Creek, and said women had, on one or more occasions, engaged in some form of sexual congress with the Chadster, and they were receiving these checks for that reason, he had copies of these checks with Charles Peaborne's self-important flourish of a signature right smack on the bottom of them.

Rourke had obtained copies of those checks from Miguel's attorney, who was as cooperative as Miguel had been, and when he had shown these checks to Charles Peaborne and explained what the checks perhaps indicated, that was when Charles Peaborne had wet himself. This had happened at the courthouse in their first conversation. Rourke was all understanding, and had a hunch within the first few minutes that Charles Peaborne knew nothing whatever about the payoffs, but he needed at least a few more interviews to make sure. Those interviews occurred over the course of a week or ten days, during which time Peaborne lost about fifteen pounds and slept erratically, if at all. He was so eager to convince Rourke of his innocence of all monkeyshines that he actually behaved in such an odd way that it kept Rourke asking questions for an extra interview or so. But when Chad resigned, and it became apparent that no one at Camel Creek was going to pursue him for paying hush money to his former bed chums, the whole line of questioning became pointless. But by this point, Charles Peaborne had become greatly chastened by his interviews with the law, had taken down his website, gotten a job selling office supplies at Staples, and assumed what might be called a low profile, which he maintained for the rest of his life.

CHAD BLINKS A COUPLE TIMES

After such knowledge, what forgiveness? Think now
History has many cunning passages, contrived corridors
And issues.
T. S. Eliot, "Gerontion"

ABOUT FOUR WEEKS AFTER the Lester divorce was final, Brian and Michelle got married in a small ceremony with a justice of the peace. The witnesses were Shannon and Kimberly, who got on well enough with Brian, and who were happy to be sort of moving on with everything. And Brian and Michelle really were a good match-up, more or less, and got along really well together, more or less. They only had two points of conflict, and they had worked out a reasonable truce on those before the ceremony. Michelle had said that she might or might not *ever* go to church at Grace Reformed with Brian, and all she wanted was absolutely no pressure on it. And Brian had insisted that Michelle keep all her money in a separate account, protected by a prenup that he had had his own attorney draw up. He had done this, he told Michelle, because he did not want to be seen in any way by anyone as a money grubber. He had plenty of his own anyway. The second reason for it, which he had not yet explained to Michelle, was that he was still uncomfortable with how she had gotten the bulk of that money from Chad. They had talked about both issues, about the church and the prenup, and had agreed to just leave it there. The ceremony was nice.

The fact that Brian Lewis had been attending Grace Reformed intermittently was evidence that he was caught up in what might be called a slow-build spiritual crisis. Not like St. Paul, who, by most accounts, was blown off his horse all at once, Brian had always been thoughtful and deliberate about spiritual things, and he had been assembling the pieces for a number of years. He had been very diligent in his own way, but he was like a guy putting together a jigsaw puzzle of a lighthouse, but one where things got mixed up in the closet, and the picture on the box lid was that of a sailing boat. He was diligent, but was making slow progress.

After the wedding, he continued to attend church, only more regularly than before. It got to the point where he was attending virtually every Sunday. Then one Sunday something just snapped, and he saw that it was supposed to be a lighthouse, not a sailing boat, for pity's sake. John Mitchell had gotten to the text about bringing every thought to the "obedience of Christ," and Brian felt like he had been watching a blurry, out-of-focus movie for an hour and a half, and then someone had adjusted the focus for him with fifteen minutes left in the film. Everything made sense. Absolutely *everything*, even the first part of the movie, which he would have to watch over again in his head. Brian talked to John after the service, told him what had happened during the sermon, and asked about baptism.

John told Brian to take care that he not go off and buy a fifty-pound Bible in order to go home and tell Michelle he'd been saved. "Keep your mouth shut unless she asks." Okay, why? John explained why. "We'll set up the baptism for you. You should invite her to that, but I bet she asks you what happened before you have to bring it up. Trust me."

/ / / / / /

Chad Lester was living a crumpled-up little life in his condo on the south side. He didn't go out much. He had money to live on, but not enough to do anything in the grand style, and not enough to undertake any monumental projects. He didn't *feel* like any monumental projects. He had fired all his attorneys and rearranged his remaining affairs somewhat lethargically so that he would continue to have something to do. After three months or so, he gave his book agent an exhortation about doing "something." The *Walking With Christ Through Divorce* book had been pulled by the publisher after a raucous board meeting, at which some of the PR people had brought up *Trolling for Chicks With Christ Through Divorce*, a website for "struggling pastors" who needed to learn how to "score."

"Is this for real?" one of the elderly board members asked, a fellow who didn't get out much.

"No, it is not for real, Mr. Gerahty," said someone from marketing. "It is a satiric website. Legal department said there is nothing we can do, except not publish the book. Which they recommend, by the way. The kill fee is a lot less than what we would likely have to pay in new and interesting ways if we go ahead."

That was the eventual decision, with the remarkable thing being that it took so long. Chad Lester had received the news with apathy and was in no frame of mind to fight them over it. But after a few months, his mind began to turn toward other book projects, just for something to do, and hence the exhortation to his agent. His agent was working on a project for him, but said that he couldn't do much until he had a hook or something. "You losing your faith? Recovering it? In between? I gotta know who to call, Chad."

But Chad would mostly sit, try to write, watch television, and go to the grocery store once a week. There was an occasional woman overnight, but he didn't have the star power he used to, and for some reason, he didn't have all the same compulsions he used to have. The same thing was true of the booze and the porn. And the women he slept with—three of them, actually—were alumni who thought that he probably still had a lot of money, which he didn't, at least when compared to before. He was just plain bored. He started going to a neighborhood Episcopal church once a week as well. The vicarette there was a radical lesbo-priestess, but she still did the early service right out of the Book of Common Prayer, nobody being exactly sure why.

Chad didn't listen to her homilies—he was too good a smoke-blower himself not to see right through what she was doing.

So he just sat, not paying attention to much of anything. But occasionally a phrase from the prayer book would create a little spiritual *thruppa-da-da,* much like what happens when you forget to put the lawn mower in the garage for the winter, and try to get it started in the spring. Nothing much there, but occasionally there might be a noise that might indicate that at some point in the indefinite future there *might* be something there. Every three weeks or so, the Rev. Jane Hutchens, for that was her name, would read something profound that Thomas Cranmer had written in the sixteenth century, Lord knows why anymore, and Chad would shift in his seat. *Thruppa-da-da.*

He didn't think about it much though. He would just go home afterward and sit. Then read a bit. Then channel surf. Then he would try to write. But mostly the lawn mower just sat there, and no grass actually got cut.

/ / / / / /

It had taken Michelle a week and a half to ask Brian what had happened to him. She had noticed after a day and a half, but waited to see if he was going to say something. When he didn't, she finally got up the nerve to ask. "Brian, what happened? You have been . . . so pleasant."

He laughed. "Was I that unpleasant?"

"No, *no.* You were fine. I just don't know what else to call it."

So he told her and said that his baptism was two weeks away. "I would like to invite you and the girls to come . . . but I don't want to pressure you . . . I want to honor our deal."

"Oh, no . . . I would be glad to come for your baptism." Michelle was actually glad for a face-saving reason to break the ice and attend Grace Reformed. She had been growing increasingly curious, but out of pride had not wanted to ask. And this was just plain weird. She had felt a little guilty about marrying someone without a testimony, but this seemed very different from the testimonies she was used to. But at least it was *some* kind of a testimony, she told herself.

The service upended her. She had never heard or seen anything like it. At the conclusion of the service, the congregation sang a few hymns while John and Brian were getting ready in the back. After the songs, a little maroon curtain, behind the place where the choir usually stood, came open with two or three herky-jerky motions. Michelle's first impulse was to laugh because the little rectangle with two people in it looked like one of those old Punch and Judy shows. But when she saw the expression on Brian's face, she swallowed hard and teared up, not knowing why.

The girls had come also and pretended to act like that one service was all they needed. But what had really happened is that they saw their counselor, Stefan MacDonald, in the foyer after the service and were really pleased to see him, but they also thought that they should act like they were really weirded out by it. At least for the time being.

Michelle, without saying anything, began attending with Brian. He was pleased, but decided not to press his luck by asking her about it. After a month or two of *that*, the same thing happened to her that had happened to Brian. When the idea of repenting had first begun occurring to her, she had thought it would involve a few outstanding big-ticket items. Her divorce, her adultery, and maybe the money she had sneeveled away from Chad. But when it finally happened to her, the whole thing was far more illuminating than she had thought it would be and went all the way back to her girlhood. Vanity, selfishness, conceit, superficiality, covetousness, ambition—all of them tumbled off the top bookshelf of her mind and were just lying there on the floor, waiting for someone to pick them all up and throw them away.

Brian saw right away what had happened to her, and urged her to make an appointment with John Mitchell to ask him what she should do. In the aftermath, one of the first things she had brought up with Brian was Chad's money, and he said "You need to ask John." All her prejudices against John had vanished by this point, as had all his concern about her—an old flame from afar—being in his congregation. This wasn't junior high, and Cindi had made friends with Michelle right away. Matters were helped along by the fact that Michelle had absolutely no recollection of John Mitchell going to school with her.

She made the appointment, and one of the first things she did was throw John a major-league sinker, starting high and inside and ending just above the knees. She explained about the money and said, "You know, the *money* is really not important. I think that I ought to return a bunch of it to him, and I have no problem with that, but that is not what bothers me. What bothers me is that I will have to *talk* to him. Sometimes I think I have forgiven him, and other times the thought of talking to him without fighting just creeps me out. I don't know how to talk to that man without being angry. I haven't done it for years."

John sat there for a moment, scratching his beard, trying to look judicious and wise. *You and me both, sister,* he was thinking. But pastors don't have the option of saying things like, "This particular sin has me by the throat too. Nothing whatever can be done about it. Go away." And so he told her what he had told many others—all about the nature and practice of forgiveness. But this was a *unique* sort of forgiveness—a kind of *Chad*-forgiveness—that he had never had to deal with before. Still, the teaching he laid out made sense, at least to Michelle, and it appeared to be a great help to her. "Okay, I'll do it," she said and got up to go. "Thank you so much," she said and disappeared.

John just sat, staring at the wall. *The only way, as I see it, John,* he said to himself, *to avoid a charge of thundering hypocrisy is for you to go do the same thing. You need to square things with him on a number of levels. The black eye, believing Cherie's story, hating him in a high pharisaical dudgeon for years,* sheesh. In his mind, John went over the passages he had shown to Michelle. *Nope. No way out. Don't want to do it, though. Still don't want to do it. What could I do to make a living if I left the pastorate?*

/ / / / / /

Three days later, Michelle pulled up and parked in the street outside Chad's condo. She looked in her purse. The *sizable* check was still there. She swallowed hard, prayed, and got out. She rang the doorbell and hoped that Chad was not going to be there. She could always do this tomorrow. But Chad was there, as evidenced by him opening the door and standing there startled.

"Hello," Michelle said.

"Uh, hello," Chad said.

"Do you have a minute to talk?"

"Um, yeah, sure. Come in."

She did, and sat down on an offered chair. Chad gestured helplessly. "To what do I owe this . . . um, visit?" he asked.

The first thing she did was hand him the check, like Jacob driving his flocks toward Esau, not that either of them was thinking about this exactly. He looked at the check in genuine surprise. "What . . . what?" he said.

"Well," she said, "I had a change of heart over what I did in the divorce." She was over the hump. "Not a change of mind, a change of *heart*. Our marriage was a mess, and I am not here to talk about anything that you did in it. I . . . I just need to seek your forgiveness for . . ." She was trying to find the Bible word, and realized there probably wasn't one. ". . . for being such a bitch. When your dad died. There was a bunch of other stuff too, and I am so sorry for all of it. Please forgive me."

Chad was unstrung and could play no tune. "Okay," he said. He didn't say anything like, "Me, I'm sorry too for being ten times worse," but she could see that it was just because he was so surprised. If he had been able to put his feelings into words, it would have been something like, "What happened to *you?*" But he wasn't, and he didn't.

"Well, that's it," she said. "Thanks for talking with me."

He showed her to the door and then walked back to his living room, looking at the check and scratching his head. He sat down on the sofa. There was something funny going on here. He resolved to pay closer attention to the prayer-book readings next Sunday. Maybe God was trying to tell him something. He just sat there for about twenty minutes and was then startled to hear someone else at the door. When he opened it, there was John Mitchell.

/ / / / / /

John had followed GPS directions to get there, which is why he had not arrived in the middle of Michelle's visit. Some GPS programs still had some work to do when it came to construction projects. So he was already mildly annoyed, but it was not because he had gotten slightly lost. It was because he was going to talk to Chad, and he was looking for other reasons to be annoyed.

He pulled into the parking spot and pulled on the emergency brake a little too hard. Again, it came off in his hand—just like that night at Cherie's apartment. He stared at it with malice. Here was an inanimate object that he could be angry with safely. He had taken the car into the shop after he had broken the emergency brake the last time, and they had clearly pretended to fix it. Sixty dollars' worth of fixing was sitting there in his hand, staring back up at him insolently. *Do you do well to be angry?* came into his head, but he was not sure why.

"Yes, I *do*," he shouted at the parking brake handle. A lady walking by with a double stroller looked at him with alarm. He tried to grin at her through the windshield. *Sorry, lady.* She hastened her step and disappeared down the sidewalk. *Two little kids,* John thought. *Who don't know their right hand from their left,* he added to himself. And then he began to laugh uncontrollably, longer than it seemed possible. Another couple passersby glanced into the car with concern, but John didn't care anymore. He laughed until he was almost sick, and when he was done, he was at peace. *All done with that,* he thought, and got out of the car and ran up the stairs two at a time to Chad's front door.

He rang the bell and waited patiently. After just a moment, Chad Lester was standing in the open doorway. John held both his hands up, palms facing toward Chad. "I come in peace," he said.

Chad stepped back. "Come in," he said. This was his day for surprises.

He ushered John into his living room, offered him a drink, which John declined, and they both sat down.

"Well," John said, when the moment came, "I am here to ask your forgiveness for several things. There are a couple particular things and one general thing. May I?"

Chad was feeling really awkward. He had not had a moment to process Michelle's request for forgiveness, and here was somebody else, doing it *again*. But he nodded anyway.

John Mitchell had rehearsed what he was going to say about fifty times, and he was a preacher, good with words. But he was still not sure how it was going to come out. "I need to seek your forgiveness for believing Cherie's lie about you. I wanted to believe it. It fit into everything I had come to believe about you. Please forgive me."

Chad nodded. "You know that Cherie lied?"

"My wife and I figured that out later. But yes, we know that she lied. She was getting revenge from . . . from before."

A moment passed without either man saying anything. Then John spoke again. "Because I believed that lie, and because of the state of my heart, I completely overreacted when you stumbled and fell into me. Please forgive me for giving you that black eye."

Chad's hand instinctively went to his face. Traces of the shiner had been with him for weeks. He nodded again.

"This third thing," John said, "is the most humiliating to me because I knew better. Scripture says to be angry without sinning, and to not let the sun go down on your anger. I got angry over your treatment of Cherie years ago, which was fine, but that kind of anger is like manna. Even if it is good, it goes bad overnight if you try to keep it. I let the sun go down on it, and when I woke up, I detested you. And I have detested you ever since that time. Until today. Would you please forgive me for that?"

Chad was looking at the backs of both his hands. He turned them slowly and spoke, just as slowly. "Michelle was just here," he said. "She did something very similar to what you are doing.

I did not know what would be appropriate to say to her, and I certainly do not know what to say to you. But I know these are big things. This is a big deal." He looked up. "If I knew, I would do it. Can that suffice?"

John smiled. This was the part he wasn't sure he could do. But after he asked forgiveness, it just fell into place. "That will do fine. One more thing. Can I call you from time to time so we can grab a beer together?"

"I would like that," Chad said.

Thruppa-da-da.

BUT I LOVE TO WATCH YOU GO

I have eaten my honeycomb with my honey;
I have drunk my wine with my milk: eat, O friends;
drink, yea, drink abundantly, O beloved.
Canticles v.i

JOHN MITCHELL PULLED HIS FEET off the desk and extended his left hand to Cindi, who came into his study and sat on his lap.

"Are you sure you have to go to the baby shower tonight?"

"I'm sure," she said.

"I hate it when you leave me."

"You're a dear . . . why do you always say that?"

John had been waiting for her to ask, and it had only taken three months. "It's from an old blues song I heard on the radio."

She snuggled down closer to him. He reached up and began to stroke her neck with his finger, the way she liked it. "You be *careful*," she said.

"Why?" he said. He thought this was a reasonable question.

"I think Sandy might still be here. We have children."

He grinned and breathed in her ear. "Do you know *why* we have children?"

She pushed against his chest, a little halfheartedly, and sat up. "Do you like my hair like this?"

"I love it when you wear it up like that," he said earnestly. "Your barrettes are twin fawns grazing among the lilies."

"You are in a *state*," she said. "How does the rest of that blues song go?"

"It is similar to Adam's sentiment in *Paradise Lost*—'Her long, with ardent look, with eye pursued, delighted, but desiring more her stay.'"

"Right. But what does the song say?"

"I hate it when you leave me, but I love to watch you go."

Cindi jumped to her feet, but it was clear she had taken no offense. This was a dance they both knew the steps to. "You are absolutely *impossible*," she said, and out the door of the study she went. But there was a little extra swing in it for him.

John sat quietly at his desk, fiddled around with his commentaries, and tried to think Second Corinthianish thoughts. It wasn't working very well. All he could think about was the fact that Cindi was mistaken. Sandy wouldn't be home for a couple more hours—Sandy had told him that herself. And Cindi would be out late at the stupid baby shower. This was an ardent lover's chance of a lifetime. Or of the week, maybe.

With a sigh that fooled nobody, had anyone been there, John put his books down and headed off to the kitchen. It was time to lift Cindi's ponytail up and nibble on the back of her neck. To pretend to make up for quoting that song.

Many thanks to Tim Travaglini.